I0598965

Jake Stellar
Beach Shoot

Jake Stellar

Beach Shoot

By

Rodney Riesel

Published by Island Holiday Publishing

East Greenbush, NY

ISBN: 978-0-9894877-5-7

First Edition

Special thanks to:

Pamela Guerriere

Kevin Cook

Cover Photo Copyright:

http://www.123rf.com/profile_vadmary'>vadmary /
123RF Stock Photo</a>

Cover Design by:

Connie Fitsik

To learn about my other books friend me at

https://www.facebook.com/rodneyriesel

**For Brenda,
Kayleigh, Ethan
& Peyton**

Chapter One

I pulled on my running shorts and sat on the edge of the bed to tie my sneakers. It was much more comfortable to stand and put one shoe on the bed to tie them, but Bree might walk into the room at any minute and who wants to listen to that speech again? I had done it a hundred times with no incident but the one time she walks into the room was the one time I had oil or grease, or something on the bottom of my shoe. What the Christ is a duvet anyway? It looked like a blanket to me. Sure, maybe it was foolish to put my shoes on the bed, but not as foolish as spending $270 on a blanket.

"You better not have your shoes on the bed," Bree said as she walked into the room and grabbed her jacket off of the closet doorknob.

"What kind of a moron would do that," I asked innocently.

She slipped on her jacket. "I only know one kind."

"You're wearing a jacket?" I asked.

"It's chilly."

It *was* a little chilly for September, but I was only wearing a short sleeve T-shirt. Tough and rugged, that's me.

"You'll be taking it off halfway through the run," I informed her.

"Maybe, Maybe not. How far did you want to go?" she asked.

"Six or seven miles, maybe."

"Well, look at you! Drop a few pounds, and all of the sudden you're an Olympic runner. What's next, the Myrtle Beach Marathon?"

I knew she was picking on me for my recent foray into a slightly healthier lifestyle, but getting shot and having a butcher knife shoved into my side had scared me shitless. I had started eating a little better, I lost a few pounds, and I was running more. Nothing makes you want to live more than being scared you're going to die.

Bree walked out through the garage into the driveway. I followed, lifting my face toward the sun. It felt good. *I* felt good.

I glanced over at Bree; she was bent over and touching her toes with very little effort. I didn't even try. Instead, I walked out to the curb to stretch my calves and hamstrings.

After a few more minutes of stretching she asked, "Ready?"

"Ready when you are." We kissed and said I love you, as we usually do before a run, because who knows? I might have a massive coronary and hit the road halfway through. After all, I am almost fifty. I glanced down at my watch: 8:52.

Bree turned and quickly rounded the corner onto Hillside Drive.

I had always enjoyed running, but it had been even more enjoyable these last couple of months being able to run alongside of Bree rather than struggling along like the fat little engine that couldn't twenty feet behind her. Don't get me wrong, the view was much better running behind than beside her, but being able to keep up is way better.

We ran along Hillside all the way to Main Street and took a right toward the beach. We made our way through the public access and onto the sand.

When we were almost back to the Bay Watch Resort, Bree announced, "That's enough for me," and slowed to a walk. Some women glistened, or so they say; Bree sweated. And it looked damn good on her. I watched her shed her jacket and toss it on the sand.

"Too hot for the jacket, huh?"

"Smart ass." She took off her shoes and socks and waded out into the ocean up to her ankles. "How far do you think that was?"

"A little over five, I would guess." Five miles and I was barely panting. Pushing fifty wasn't fatal after all. Feeling my oats, I kicked off my shoes, too, and joined her in the water.

"Looks like it's going to be a beautiful day," she said. "Maybe we should make this a beach day."

"Sounds good to me." I reached inside my pocket to make sure I still had my money.

"How much money do you have on you?" Bree asked.

"About eight bucks. Why?"

"You want to walk back up the beach and get coffee someplace?"

"Sure."

We had made it back to Seventeenth Avenue when we noticed a photographer setting up his tripod in the sand. His other equipment lay at his feet in a black leather bag. I had seen this shutterbug, middle-aged hipster type, before. He was one of several who took snaps of locals and tourists on the perfect backdrop of the beach.

"Good morning," I said cordially, improvising a little two-fingered salute.

He smiled at Bree and me. "What's up, folks?"

"Not his blood pressure, thank God," Bree said with a smirk.

We made a slight turn and headed up to the Seventeenth Avenue public access path. When we got to the small parking area next to Molly Darcy's Irish Pub, a black Ford Explorer pulled into a spot. A father, mother, and four children, two boys and two girls, ranging in age from five to twelve, climbed from the vehicle. The entire family was dressed in blue jeans and white, long-sleeved shirts with button-down collars. Matching flip-flops completed the crisp, clean family uniform.

We stepped to the side and let them pass. The mother was wetting her fingers with her tongue and trying to tame the youngest boy's cowlick. The oldest boy and girl were shoving each other as they walked along.

"Knock it off!" the dad said, and glanced at me with that *somebody save me* look.

The mother was still fussing with the tyke's hair. "You want to look handsome for our family portrait, don't you?"

she fretted. "The nice photographer's going to take our picture on the beach. Won't that be fun?"

"No, it won't be fun," the little boy sulked. "It'll be *sissy*."

"Oh you hush up!" the mom said and gave his bottom a playful whack.

Bree watched as the little guy walked by her. He looked up and smiled. Bree smiled back and watched as he made his way down the path and onto the sand. I knew what she was thinking, because I was thinking it, too. This boy was about the same age as our son Ricky when we lost him.

I always found it strange that when you buy a new car, suddenly half the cars on the road seem to be the same model as yours. You never noticed there were so many of them before. The same thing goes when you lose a child. Suddenly everyone seems to have a little boy the same age yours was. *Was*. It still hurt to think of Ricky in the past tense.

We made it through the parking lot and turned right onto Ocean Boulevard. Bree was quiet. I tried to make conversation. "It *is* a nice day." Like we hadn't already talked about that.

"Yup," she mumbled.

We crossed the street, and as I looked to my left for traffic, a tan, late model Chevy Malibu was barreling toward us. I grabbed Bree's arm and pulled her back to the curb, but the Chevy took a right into the parking lot before reaching us. We crossed. I shot the speed demon a mental bird.

We had almost made it to Sixteenth Avenue when we heard four loud pops and someone scream. Bree and I looked at each other.

We heard tires squeal and as I looked back the way we came, that same Chevy Malibu was speeding across Ocean Boulevard toward North Kings Highway.

"Come on!" I shouted, and we ran down the Sixteenth Avenue access.

When we got to the beach, I looked toward the photographer. His eyes were wide, and his jaw was practically on his chest. Someone was lying in the sand, and a few others had gathered around. We sprinted toward them.

"Do you have your cell phone?" I asked.

"No," Bree answered.

"Me neither."

When we reached the group, we saw the mother from earlier lying on the ground on her back, her new white shirt now stained red, and the stain was growing. The father was kneeling over her. "Hang on, Emily, hang on, Emily," he kept repeating.

The four children were huddled together in a little knot, craning their heads for a better look at a scene they couldn't comprehend. I looked at the photographer and a woman standing next to him and shouted. "Get these kids out of here!"

The husband was too dazed to be of any real help. Taking charge, Bree dropped to her knees and yanked off her T-shirt, wadded it up, and pressed it against the woman's wound. I realized Bree had forgotten her jacket, and in the same split second I thought how sexy she looked in just a sports bra. Funny how your mind works in a crisis.

"Does anyone have a cell phone?" I asked. When I looked up, I saw that two people did; the jackals were using them to record the incident. I reached for one of the phones and the guy jerked it away from me. I stood, grabbed the phone, and shoved him backwards; he landed on his ass in the sand.

I slapped the other cell phone from the second man's hand and then dialed 911.

"This is Detective Jake Stellar. We have a shooting on the beach at the Seventeenth Avenue access. I need an ambulance." The 911 operator started to say something, but I dropped the phone into the sand.

I looked down at Bree; she had just finished mouth-to-mouth and was starting chest compressions. She looked up at me and gently shook her head no.

Chapter Two

Pat Murray and his new partner, Ronnie Pierce were the first responders on the scene. Together they had driven several wooden stakes in the sand and roped off the entire area of the beach with yellow plastic caution tape. They had used the same tape to block off the entrance to the parking lot, as well as the access path.

Detective Gwen Lawrence was speaking with the victim's husband. Gwen's partner, Dill Perkins, was questioning the photographer. A female uniform stood next to a bench where all four children were seated. They were fidgety, scared, and confused. I could tell by the expression on her face that she was awkwardly trying to keep the children occupied. *Good luck*, I thought.

The rear door of the coroner's van slammed shut. I glanced over. Bree was with the coroner. She was still shirtless, and knowing her, not feeling very comfortable in just a sports bra. Seeing how she had her arms crossed self-consciously across her chest, I removed my shirt and walked toward her. I didn't feel very comfortable being shirtless either, especially around my coworkers.

"I always knew you would give me the shirt off your back," Bree said, and slipped on my shirt. It just about swallowed her petite torso.

"I wouldn't have to, if you hadn't left your jacket on the beach."

"I did? Yeah, I guess I did. Everything's a blur."

Gwen was done with the husband, and he joined his children at the bench, gathering them into a group hug. Gwen met up with me on the access path.

"Casual Sunday?" Gwen asked, referring to my outfit.

"When ya got it, flaunt it," I responded.

"The husband said he didn't see anything."

"Someone walked up to his family and shot his wife, and he didn't see anything. How's that possible?" I asked.

"It happened so quickly. He said he was tucking in his son's shirt when he heard the pops. At first, he thought it was firecrackers. When he looked up, his wife fell to the ground. By the time he realized what had happened, he heard the squeal of the tires."

"Photographer see anything?" I asked Dill.

"He said by the time he looked up, the guy was already climbing back into his vehicle, so he didn't get a look at his face," Dill explained. "He got a good look at the vehicle, though."

"So did I," I said. "Tan Malibu. Late model. Two-door."

"You're three for three, Jake," Dill said, grinning. "The shell casings were found right here." He pointed to where the sand met the blacktop. "So he fired from pretty far away. Probably why no one got a good look at him."

Beach Shoot

"No one got a good look," I pointed out. "but everyone keeps saying, 'him'."

Pat Murray was walking toward us and overheard my observation. "Let's hope North Myrtle Beach hasn't gotten so depraved that the shooter's a female," he said with a sigh. "But you're right, Jake. Everyone seems to be able to describe the car, but no one can describe the driver," he added.

I pointed at the two bargain basement paparazzi that had been recording the scene. "Pat, make sure you get those two guys phones__, might be something on there."

"Will do," he replied and made his way toward them.

I watched as Pat reached the two men. Neither was too happy to give up their precious smart phones. It didn't seem to matter that some guy had just lost his wife. *Assholes.*

The coroner climbed in his van and sped off. Bree walked over to where the children were seated. She took the youngest boy's hand in one of hers and wiped the tears from his cheeks with the other. I wondered what she was telling him. When I reached her, she stood, gave the boy a smile; he smiled back. His oldest sister put her arm around him and squeezed as he buried his face in her arm.

Bree turned to the father and said, "I'm so sorry for your loss." He nodded.

Together, Bree and I walked over to Gwen. "I'm going to head on home, take a shower, and get dressed," I advised her. "I'll be in in a couple of hours." I looked at my watch. "See if the husband can come down to the station around noon to answer a few questions."

"Kind of soon, isn't it?" she asked.

"Better to talk to him while it's all fresh in his mind."

She agreed, and Bree and I made our way across the parking lot.

"You want a ride?" Pat called out.

"Nah."

Bree reached over and took my hand. "I love you," she said.

"Who wouldn't?" I asked. "Look at me, walking along with no shirt on. They should put me on the North Myrtle Beach cop calendar, for Christ sakes."

"They have one of those?"

"No, but you can bet I'll be dropping that note into the suggestion box when I get to the station."

Chapter Three

Christopher Bowen sat on a dark brown leather sofa in the lounge at the North Myrtle Beach police department. His eyes were red, his face pale. He looked ten years older than he had the first time I had seen him, in the parking lot that same morning, a morning that had started out as a family day but had ended with one less family member.

The lounge was a much more comfortable place to question someone involved in a crime. It wasn't as cold and sterile feeling as the interrogation room. The lighting was softer, the room warmer.

"Can I get you a cup of coffee, Mr. Bowen?" Gwen asked.

"Yes, thank you," he answered. He rubbed his eyes for what was probably the millionth time today.

I sat quietly in a chair that matched the sofa as Gwen poured the coffee.

"Cream or sugar?"

"Black, please."

Gwen handed Bowen the cup; he blew on it and took a sip.

"Mr. Bowen, I know this is hard for you," Gwen said, as she took a seat in another chair next to mine. "But we just have to ask you a few more questions."

"I don't know what more I could tell you. I already explained to the other detective that I didn't see the man. I … I was helping get the children ready for our family portrait." He paused, dropped his head, and rubbed his eyes again. "I'm sorry, this is just so—"

"Take your time, Mr. Bowen," Gwen said.

I waited a few seconds for him to regain his composure. "Has your wife had any problems at work lately?" I asked. "Maybe with one of the other teachers, or a student?"

He shook his head. "No. I mean, not that she's mentioned. Why, do you think someone Emily works with could have done this?"

"We can't rule anything out at this point, Mr. Bowen," Gwen explained.

"Please, call me Chris."

There was a knock at the door, and Captain Merle Stein poked his head into the room. As usual he was wearing a white dress shirt with a button-down collar. I immediately thought of Bowen's family, and how they had all dressed in matching shirts for their photo shoot. I wondered if Bowen was thinking the same thing.

"Can I talk to you for a second?" Merle asked.

"Sure." I got up, and he held the door for me as I left the room and shut it behind me.

"What's up, Cap'n?" I asked.

"They found the Malibu abandoned at the end of Atlantic Street in a parking lot," Merle said. "I've got a couple of units over there now, knocking on doors. Crime scene is there, going over the car. It's registered to a Larry Davis." Merle looked down at the paper he was holding. "He lives at 874 Anne Street."

"Did you send anyone over?" I asked.

"Yeah. No one was home. Now here's the kicker: The vehicle was reported stolen right around the time we found it."

"Of course it was." I took the paper from him. "Okay, thanks," I said, and returned to the lounge. Bowen watched me as I crossed the room and took my seat. I could see in his eyes he was waiting for me to give him some good news. I didn't have any.

"We found the car abandoned in a parking lot at the end of Atlantic Street, Chris," I told him. "Do you know anyone that might live in that area?"

"No. I can't think of anyone."

I turned to Gwen. "Get a list of Mrs. Bowen's students, as well as the faculty … and their addresses."

"You got it," Gwen said and left the room.

I leaned forward in my chair and rested my elbows on my lap. "Chris, I'm going to ask you some questions you're not going to want to hear, and you might not even want to answer. But please understand, I have to ask them."

"I understand," he said.

"Have you and your wife had any problems lately? Have you been arguing more than usual?"

He shook his head no to both questions. "Detective, my wife and I barely argue. I know that might sound hard for some people to believe, but we get along … we *got* along … very well. I can't even remember the last time we had a fight. Emily was a good person; she didn't deserve this. I can't imagine why anyone would have done this to her."

I stared for a moment into Bowen's eyes. Either he had a great marriage, or he was a great actor. I didn't think there was any reason to ask him any of the other questions I had, because if he and his wife really were as blissfully happy as Ward and June Cleaver I wouldn't get the answers I was looking for, and if they weren't, then he probably wouldn't tell me the truth.

I stood and motioned toward the door. "I believe you, Chris. We'll be in contact."

I watched Bowen as he lumbered down the hall and out the front door of the police station. Merle walked up beside me. "Learn anything?" he asked.

"There's one less perfect marriage in the world," I responded.

"I didn't know there was any such thing as a perfect marriage."

"There's not."

Chapter Four

When I got to the end of Atlantic Street, I pulled to the curb and parked. Perkins was already at the scene and had the entire parking lot taped off. The same two-door Malibu I had seen earlier in the day was parked close to the middle of the parking lot; both doors and the trunk were open.

Perkins met me at the rear of the car. "How's things going here?" I asked.

"Crime scene lifted some prints from inside the car, and they found footprints leading away from the car. The prints head north and go as far as Twenty-Eighth Avenue, near the water tower, and end," Perkins explained, pointing toward the North Myrtle Beach water tower looming in the distance, like an oversized golf tee with a big white ball on top. "He must have had a car waiting there for him."

"What did CSU say about the footprints?" I asked, looking down at the trail.

"No make on the shoe but it's a size ten and a half and judging from the stride and indent of the toe, the driver is between five-ten and six-one. He was running, and he weighs about 175."

"Did they get his hair color, too?" I joked.

Perkins gave me a half grin. "Uniforms went door to door, but no one noticed the car even sitting here. The trees block any view from the south," he said, and then pointed at some houses to the west. "The houses over there all face the other direction."

"A well-thought-out getaway."

"You think it was a professional?"

"I can't imagine it would be. What could a high school teacher and mother have done to attract the attention of a professional hit man? Probably just someone who knew the area well."

"Did you get anything from the husband?"

"Just that his wife should have been nominated for sainthood," I said sarcastically.

Perkins turned. "I'm going to touch base with the uniforms and then head back to the station."

"When you get there, pull up the Bowen's finances; let's see if there are any flaws in their flawless life."

Perkins turned back and lowered his brow. "What's with all the pessimism?"

I shrugged my shoulders. "I don't know. I just find it hard to believe that someone went through all this trouble to kill someone so perfect."

"Not everyone is hiding something, Jake."

"Yeah they are," I said, and turned toward my car. "I'm going to stop by the Davis residence on my way home."

Beach Shoot

After leaving Perkins, I took a right off of North Kings Highway onto Twenty-Seventh Avenue and drove around by the water tower. A unit was parked at the edge of the street. An officer was leaning up against the car, smoking a cigarette. When he saw me, he pushed himself away from the car and tossed the cigarette into the dirt.

There were sawhorses placed around the site and the usual plastic yellow tape went from horse to horse. As I drove by, I couldn't resist lowering the power window and asking rhetorically, "Working hard or hardly working? He nodded back with a sheepish grin.

I pulled into the driveway at 874 Anne Street and stopped behind a white Chevy Trail Blazer.

When I knocked on the door, a young man dressed in red gym shorts and a black T-shirt answered.

"Yeah?" he said rudely, with the kind of look on his face you would love to remove with the back of your hand.

I looked him up and down. *He's between five-ten and six-one and weighs about 175*, I thought. *I should just shoot him now.* Not because I thought he killed anyone, but because he's a wiseass teenager.

"I'm detective Jake Stellar with the North Myrtle Beach Police Department. Are your parents at home?"

He snorted. "Jake Stellar, sounds like a lame TV cop."

You're pushing it, asshole. "I've never heard that one before. Are your parents home?"

"Sure, hold on," he said and walked away, leaving the door open. I figured that was his way of inviting me in, so I stepped into the foyer and closed the door behind me.

A few seconds later, I was approached by a man that was obviously the boy's father. He had the same build and the same hair color, but peppered with gray. He stuck out his hand when he reached me. "Larry Davis," he announced.

I shook his hand. "Detective Jake Stellar. I understand you had your vehicle stolen this morning."

"Yes." He turned and motioned for me to follow. "Would you like a cup of coffee, Detective?"

A cup of coffee actually sounded really good. "Yes, please."

I followed him into the kitchen. "Have a seat," he said.

I sat while he poured coffee into a mug that was already sitting on the countertop. Then he grabbed another mug from the cupboard and poured my coffee.

I said, "Thank you," and he took the chair across from me.

He took a sip. "Yeah, someone stole the car right out of the driveway. What's happening to this area? When we first moved here, we didn't even worry about locking our house doors, much less the car doors."

"When was the last time you drove the car, Mr. Davis?"

"Oh I never drive it; it's my son's car."

"The boy who answered the door?"

"Yes."

"Can I speak with him, also, please?"

"Jeremy!" Davis shouted. "Come in here for a second."

"What?" Jeremy hollered back.

"Get your ass in here, that's what." Davis shook his head. "Kids."

Jeremy slouched into the room. "Yeah?" you could cut the sullen in his tone with a knife.

"The detective wants to ask you a few questions."

"Yeah, what?"

I thought about asking him why he was such a douche, but decided to stick with the usual questions. "When was the last time you drove your car?"

"Last night."

"What time did you get home?"

He looked at his dad. "Midnight."

"Twelve thirty-five," Davis corrected.

"Twelve thirty-five," Jeremy agreed.

"When did you notice it missing from the driveway?" I asked.

"I got up to pee around eleven-thirty this morning. When I looked out the window, I noticed it wasn't there, so I told my dad."

"Did you leave the keys in the car?"

"No. But I left the doors unlocked, and the ignition is busted, so you don't need a key any ways. You just turn it and it starts."

"An officer stopped by a little after noon," I said. "He knocked on the door, but no one answered."

"My wife and I had gone to the grocery store," Davis said.

"And where were you, Jeremy?"

"I, uh … went back to bed. Probably fell asleep and didn't hear the doorbell."

"Kid sleeps through anything," Davis added.

"Mr. Davis, did you look in your son's room any time between nine-thirty and ten-thirty and see him sleeping?" I asked.

"No. Why?"

"Mr. Davis, your son's vehicle was used in the homicide of a forty-year-old woman this morning … about ten or twenty minutes before he says he noticed it was missing."

Davis glanced over at his son and then back at me. "You don't think my son had anything to do with killing this woman, do you?"

"I'm just asking if you can verify that he was here between nine-thirty and ten-thirty, Mr. Davis."

Davis stood. "I think we're done here, Detective."

Chapter Five

It was two in the afternoon by the time I pulled into my driveway. I hit the garage door opener on my visor. Bree's car was gone. It looked as though I would be spending the rest of my Sunday in my recliner in front of the television.

I closed the garage door behind me and went directly to the fridge, grabbed a can of ginger-ale and a bag of Nacho Cheese Doritos out of the cupboard. So much for a healthier diet, but I needed some comfort food. After using the bathroom, I settled into my chair, reclined, and opened my soda. Reaching for my remote, I turned on the television and began watching forty-three cars drive in a circle over and over and over again.

With the first sip of my soda, a thought entered my mind. It was the same thought I had every time I took that first sip: *I wonder if I could just have a couple drinks and stop*. Not a drink of soda, of course, but of Scotch, or any other alcohol for that matter. It had now been almost eight years since my last drink. I could almost still taste it. "It'll get easier," they said. They lied. I want a drink just as bad now as I did the day I quit. I opened the bag of Doritos and crammed an artificially cheesy handful into my mouth.

Watching the cars as they zoomed monotonously around Darlington Raceway was about the same as watching a gold pocket watch swing back and forth in front of your eyes, and it was having the same effect. I was getting sleepy … sleepy … sleepy. I hoped a bell didn't ring because I was in no mood to stand up, twirl in a circle, and crow like a rooster.

*****

I was startled awake when Bree tried to pull the half-empty can of Schweppes from my hand.

"What's the matter?" I asked.

She smiled. "Nothing. I just didn't want you to spill your drink." She sat the can on the end table.

I stretched and glanced at the television. *Oh look, they're still turning left.* "What time is it?"

"Almost three. Are you hungry?"

"Starving," I responded. "I haven't had anything to eat today."

"Except half a bag of Doritos." She leaned over with feigned disgust and pinched off crusted cheesy stuff from the corners of my mouth.

"There was only half a bag when I opened it."

She held out her hand, no-nonsense mother hen style, and I gave her the bag. "Who's winning?" she asked as she took a seat on the couch.

"The leader," I replied sarcastically. "You mentioned dinner."

"I didn't say anything about dinner; I asked if you were hungry."

"Well, I am."

"Well, okay."

"What are we having?"

Her eyes didn't leave the television screen. "What are you making?"

"A trip to a restaurant, I'm guessing."

"Good answer."

"Ryan's?" I suggested.

"Sounds good," she said. "Let me do something with my hair."

"They're only open till eight-thirty."

"Funny," she replied, and left the room … and took the bag of Doritos with her.

Yeah, I'm witty.

When she returned to the living room, she didn't look any different than before. "How does this look?" she asked.

"Nice," I replied. "I like your hair that way."

"What was wrong with the way it was?"

Crap. "I like it both ways," I said, not having any idea what it looked like before.

"Good answer," she said, and turned around. "Do these pants make me look fat?"

"Why, how many pairs have you eaten?"

She shook her head. "Forget it, let's go." We walked through the dining room to the door that led to the garage. "We'll have to stop and get gas, I'm on E."

"Of course you are. We'll take my truck."

"But I'll need gas in the morning."

"Then get gas in the morning."

"Why can't we just get gas now?"

"Why didn't you just get gas while you were out?"

"Because I didn't feel like stopping."

I opened the truck door and climbed in. "Neither do I." I wasn't changing my mind.

She stood next to her car, waiting for me to change my mind.

"Okay, okay," I said, as I opened my door and climbed from my truck. I walked around and got into her car. She sat facing forward with a big *I always win* grin on her face.

Chapter Six

We pulled into the Ryan's parking lot. "I think I have a coupon in here somewhere," she said unzipping her purse.

Good luck, I thought. She may as well have been searching for a certain needle in a pocketbook full of needles. I opened the car door and got out. "Come on in when you find it, and you can join me for my *second* trip to the buffet."

"Forget it." She zipped up her purse and walked across the parking lot with me.

"Huh, couldn't find it?"

"No, but I found one for Kohl's."

I pulled the door open and let Bree walk in first, which I knew she hated. "Is it good for a free buffet?"

"No, but we could go to Kohl's after we eat. I need some new running pants, and the coupon is only good until today."

"Wow, you're lucky you found that coupon," I said sarcastically.

"So, do you want to go?"

"Are you giving me a choice?"

She ignored my question.

"How are you folks tonight?" the hostess asked.

"Good," Bree answered.

"Just the two of you?"

"Yes," Bree replied, as I looked around to make sure we hadn't brought any friends that I wasn't aware of.

"Right this way."

We followed the young brunette to our table.

"Thank you," Bree said.

"I love your hair," the girl said.

"Oh, thank you."

I rolled my eyes.

"Enjoy your dinner," the hostess said as she walked away.

"At least *someone* likes my hair," Bree complained.

"That's because she didn't have to sit in the living room waiting for you to do it … without any Nacho Cheese Doritos, I might add."

"That junk's jam-packed with preservatives, you know," Bree observed.

"I know. If I keep eatin' 'em, maybe I'll live forever."

"Yeah, that would be a gift to the world."

Beach Shoot

We grabbed our plates and made our way up to the buffet. I took a piece of fried chicken, a piece of broiled fish, mashed potatoes and gravy, a biscuit, a few meatballs, and a slice of roast beef. Bree made herself a salad.

"No green or orange vegetables, I see," she said, eyeballing my heart-attack-waiting-to-happen-platter with distaste.

"Who are you, my Aunt Bee?"

When we returned to our table, our sodas were waiting for us. Bree asked, "How is the investigation going?"

I shrugged. "We have a student of hers with a shaky alibi; it was his car we saw at the scene. I spoke with the kid and his father this afternoon but the father ended the interview when I started questioning the kid's whereabouts."

She tore the paper off of her straw. "What's next?"

"I'll have them in to the station for questioning tomorrow afternoon; maybe throw a scare into the kid."

"You really think he did it?"

"To early to tell. So … new running pants, huh?" I asked to change the subject.

"You don't want to talk about it?"

"No, I just want to *eat*." I sized up my heaping plate. "Hope my eyes weren't bigger than my stomach."

Bree's eyes sparkled with that impish look I knew so well.

"Don't say it!" I warned her.

Beach Shoot

Chapter Seven

Bree had already left for work by the time I stepped out of the shower and missed her big opportunity to see me wet and naked. I figured she probably didn't mind. I got to watch *her* parade around the room after her shower, so I would have *that* image in my head all day. *She'll pay for it tonight*, I thought.

When I walked into the station, the first thing I thought was, *Oh crap, Lint's back*. I had forgotten that today was his first day back from vacation. He went to Key West for two weeks to see his daughter, Carmen, or Carla, or something__, I don't know, I wasn't really paying attention when he told me. I think he said she was from his second marriage … maybe first. I don't know and I don't care. All I know is, by the time he had left for his vacation I was glad to see him go. Merle had stuck us together for the three weeks leading up to his trip. If we had been together any longer, I might have shot him. His vacation may have saved his life.

As I walked to my desk, I couldn't take my eyes off the fat bastard. *Just look at him shoving that jelly donut into his mouth. Powdered sugar all over his face. I bet if he eats two more he would explode ... and who's going to clean up that mess? Probably need some super absorbent Bounty to clean his fat ass off the walls and ceiling.*

I removed my holster and pistol from my belt, stuck it in the top left drawer of my desk per my usual routine, and pulled out my chair.

"Stellar, want one of these jelly donuts?" Lint called out.

If I eat one I may be saving myself from the clean-up, but on the other hand, if I don't he could end up dead. Decisions, decisions. "No thanks, I ate breakfast at home," I replied.

"So did I, Stellar, but there's always room for jelly donuts."

"I think the line is, 'There's always room for Jell-O.'"

Lint look confused. "What line?"

I sat down. "Never mind."

Just as my ass touched the chair, Merle's office door swung open. "Lint, Stellar, get in here for a second."

Avis Lint hoisted his big body out of his chair with a groan. "Come on, partner," he said.

"Don't call me that." I followed Lint through the office door. "What's up, Cap'n?" I asked.

"I want you and Lint together on this Bowen homicide."

"Roger that, Cap'n," Lint blurted out.

"What about Gwen or Perkins?" I protested.

"They picked up something this morning," Merle answered. "Now get out of here and go get this guy."

"What guy?" Lint questioned.

I shook my head. "Cap'n, Perkins already knows the case. Why doesn't Lint work with Gwen today?"

Merle looked over my shoulder. "Does that say Captain Stellar on the door?"

"No," I answered in defeat.

"Then get the hell out of here."

"Ha-ha," Lint laughed. "Let's hit the bricks, partner." He turned and left the room.

"I'd like to hit you with a brick," I mumbled.

"What's that?"

"Nothing." I closed the door behind us, and we walked back to our desks. I slid open my drawer and grabbed my gun.

"What's first on the agenda, partner?" Lint inquired.

"Call me partner one more time and I'll shoot you." I clipped my holster onto my belt and turned toward the door. "Come on."

"Can I drive?"

"No."

"I have seniority."

"Then I'll let you change the tire if we get a flat."

Chapter Eight

On the ride over to North Myrtle Beach High School, I filled Lint in on the investigation as he read through my notes and looked at photographs from the crime scene. "Any questions?" I asked.

"Nope."

Of course not.

We turned off of Sea Mountain Highway and parked in the turnaround near the front entrance.

As we climbed from the car and started walking toward the door, a bandy-legged little bald man in gray Dickies stopped sweeping and stared at us.

"Good morning," I said.

"There's no parking in the circle," he grumbled back. "Gotta use the parking lot."

Lint whipped out his badge from his inside jacket pocket with a self-important flourish. "I'm Detective Avis Lint, this is Detective Jake Stellar," he proudly announced.

"Is this a police emergency?" the man asked. "Because if it's not you have to park in the parking lot."

I glanced at the name tag sewn on his shirt. Myron. *Figures*. "Myron, we're working an investigation, and we're here to speak with the principal."

"So, because you're cops you get to break the rules?"

"Yeah, we do," Lint said, as we walked by. "So why don't you record it on your pre-paid cell phone and then head over to the library with the other weirdos and post it to YouTube."

Myron had no come back for that one, but I knew we were going to hear about it later. He resumed sweeping with a vengeance, looking pissed enough to chew nails.

We stopped just inside the door to check in; I flashed *my* badge this time.

"Sign in," said the frosty old receptionist, pointing with her bony finger at a sheet attached to a clipboard. I was already the eighth person to sign in today. I wondered if the first seven received a "Good morning. How are you today?" I wondered if my taxes were paying this woman to sit here all day or if she was some kind of volunteer. I wondered how many times in her career as a sentry had she defended the school. I wondered if she would throw herself in front of an oncoming bullet to save the life of a student. I wonder too much.

"You have a nice day," I said. The crone managed a curt nod; corpses had more personality. I didn't have to ask the way to the principal's office; I assumed it was in the same place it was the last eight or nine times I had been here for something stupid. But this was my first time here for a murder.

After Lint signed in, he waddled up beside me. "How is this gonna go?" he asked.

I rolled my eyes. "I'll ask her some questions and then we'll leave."

"Sounds good," he said. "What time did you want to take lunch?"

I wondered how many times a human being could roll their eyes in one day before going permanently blind.

We walked into the office, and I flashed my shield once again. "Detective Stellar here to see Klaudia Rothstein."

Klaudia Rothstein was new this school year so I had never met her before, but I already had a mental image, from the name Klaudia. She was probably a big woman … no, very big woman, between fifty and fifty-five years old, with silver hair pulled back in a tight bun, cat eye glasses, and probably those giant quadruple D boobs that rested on her lap and stuck out as far as her knees, just like my Aunt Agnes. As I was about to enter the room, I mused that if I asked the wrong question or said the wrong thing that she would probably beat me with a yardstick.

A woman sitting at her desk behind the counter picked up her phone, punched a button, said something I couldn't hear, and then pointed at the door that said PRINCIPAL.

I opened the door and we went in.

"Good morning," Klaudia said, pushing her long brown hair behind her ear with her shiny red fingernail.

Holy crap, I thought. *Her parents should have named her Sparkles McStripper.* Her boobs were not hanging to her knees, but I think my jaw may have been. There was no principal in the continental United States that looked like this when I was a kid. If Klaudia had wings she could have been a Victoria Secret Angel.

Lint said, "Uhh."

"Good morning," I said.

43

Her eyes were as red as her fingernails; it was obvious she had been crying. We hadn't released a statement yet about Emily Bowen's murder but it was all over the news, and I would imagine that young Jeremy Davis hadn't wasted any time in running his mouth about it.

Klaudia motioned toward the chairs in front of her desk. "Please, have a seat."

"Thank you," I said.

She pulled a tissue from its beach-themed container and dabbed the inside corner of both eyes. "Sorry," she said, and then sniffed. "This is just so … so crazy."

"Mrs. Rothstein, we just have a few questions for you."

She nodded yes. "Call me Klaudia."

"Klaudia, is there anything you can tell us that would shed light on what has happened?" I asked. "Has Mrs. Bowen recently had any trouble with another member of the faculty or with any students that you can think of?"

"You think someone here may have killed her?"

"We're not jumping to any conclusions, we just have to cover all of the bases," Lint put in.

"No, but here's the list of faculty and Emily's students that you asked for," she replied, pulling the stapled-together papers from her desk drawer.

Lint took the papers. "Thank you."

"I can't think of anyone Emily had a problem with. She was one of those rare teachers that most all of the students liked. And Emily got along with everyone in faculty and administration."

Lint handed the papers to me and pointed at one of the names. "Jeremy Davis is in one of her classes," he noted.

I took the list. "How is Jeremy Davis doing in her class?"

Klaudia leaned forward and tapped a few keys on her keyboard as she stared at the computer screen. "It says here that he's in her third period English class. Report cards haven't come out yet so I'm not sure how he's doing, but he also had her last year."

"Last year?" Lint asked. "Did he fail?"

"Yes," Klaudia responded.

"Does Jeremy play sports ... track or cross country?" I asked.

"Neither of those, but he is on the football team. He's had to sit out so far this year, because of last year's failing grade."

"When is he eligible to play again?" I asked.

"As soon as report cards come out ... if he's passing."

"Can you find out for us if he's passing?"

"Yes, of course." Klaudia picked up her phone. "Andrea, can you look up the current grades for Jeremy Davis and bring them in to me? Thanks."

"We would also like to speak with his coach," I informed her.

"Certainly, his office is right down the hall."

Andrea walked in, handed Klaudia the grades, and exited. She glanced at them and handed them to me. I looked them over and saw that Jeremy was barely passing everything except English, Emily Bowen's class, which he was failing with a fifty-five.

"Thank you, Mrs. Roth—Klaudia," I said, and pulled a business card from my wallet. "Here's my cell number. If there's anything you think of later, no matter how trivial you think it is, please give me a call."

She took the card and laid it next to her phone. "I will."

"Where did you say the coach's office was?" Lint asked.

"Right down the hall. Andrea will be glad to show you the way."

Andrea led us down the hall and when we rounded the corner, she stopped and turned. "I overheard what you said to Mrs. Rothstein," she whispered. "About information, no matter how trivial it might seem."

"Yes?" I asked.

"Well, Friday after school I saw Coach Pawlak and Mrs. Bowen arguing in the teacher's parking lot."

"Do you know what they were arguing about?" Lint asked.

"I have no idea, but Coach Pawlak was spitting mad. His face was beet-red and he kept jabbing his finger at her."

Lint and I looked at each other. "Thanks, Andrea." Lint quickly removed a business card from his pocket. "If you think of anything else, don't hesitate to call me."

"I won't," she said. "And the coach's office is the one right there with the door open."

When I peeked into the coach's door, he was sitting at his desk. An athletic-looking blond girl with her hair in a ponytail stood in front of him. Her provocative body language suggested she wasn't as wholesome as she appeared. The forty-something coach had taken halfway decent care of himself and might even been handsome in his day. But a telltale hair plug job, and a wide, mean mouth set in a permanent sneer from screaming his lungs out at impressionable kids, undermined his pathetic bid for eternal youth.

"I think yoga pants are hot," the coach was saying, but stopped abruptly when he saw us. "That'll be all, Jenna."

Jenna turned and the smile abruptly left her face. "Later, Stevie," she said, as she squeezed between Lint and me and hurried down the hall.

"We didn't interrupt anything, did we, Stevie?" I asked.

He shuffled some papers around on his desk to imitate a man who was actually working. "Who are you?" he demanded.

My illustrious partner spoke up. "I'm Avis Lint and this is Jake Stellar. We're detectives with the North Myrtle Beach Police Department. We have a few questions for you."

"Jake Stellar? Wasn't that the name of a TV cop show?" Pawlak asked.

I didn't take the bait. "Mr. Pawlak, we would like to ask you a few questions about Jeremy Davis," I said.

"What about him?"

"We understand he hasn't been allowed to play football this year because of his failing English grade."

"What are you getting at, Stellar? You think he killed Bowen because of a few bad grades? I assume that's what you're talking about. Don't be ridiculous. Jeremy's a good kid. He's one of the best players I got on this team, and he's looking at a full ride from Syracuse."

"So if he doesn't play this season, the only one who stands to lose is you?" Lint asked.

"I said he was *one* of the best, not *the* best. We'll do just fine without him, assuming he doesn't bring up his grade."

"Then what were you and Mrs. Bowen arguing about in the parking lot on Friday afternoon?" I asked.

"Who told you about that?"

"Where were you yesterday morning between nine-thirty and ten-thirty, Stevie?" Lint asked.

"I was home."

"Can anyone verify that?" I asked. "Jenna, maybe?"

"What's that supposed to mean?"

"I'm just asking if anyone can verify your whereabouts while the woman you fought with on Friday was being murdered on Sunday."

"Now you think *I* had something to do with this?"

"You seem to have a bad temper," I pointed out.

"And you like to flirt with underage girls," Lint added.

"Maybe murder is the next step," I said.

Pawlak stood. I could tell by the look in his eye that if I weren't a cop, he would have come over that desk after me … I wished I wasn't a cop. "If you have any more questions, you can speak through my lawyer," he said through his clenched teeth.

Chapter Nine

We were back at the station by ten. Lint tried to get me to stop at Sonic on the way back, but luckily it wasn't open yet. I did have to promise him we would go back for lunch, though, just to shut him up.

Perkins was seated at his desk. "You and your partner having a good day?" he asked with a smirk as I walked by.

"Yeah, wonderful," I declared. "What did you and Gwen pick up?" I unclipped my holster and placed it in my desk drawer.

"Sexual assault, early this morning?" Perkins replied

"Where abouts?"

"On the beach, near the end of Main Street."

"What time did it happen?"

"A little after one."

"The victim okay?"

Perkins rocked back in his chair and laced his fingers atop his thinning scalp. "Yeah, she'll be fine. She's lucky her boyfriend came out and looked for her when he did. They were at The Pirate's Cove; she went out to the car to get something. They were parked across South Ocean Boulevard, in the parking lot at the end of Main Street. Guy grabbed her from behind and dragged her out onto the beach."

"She get a look at him?"

"Nah, he was wearing a gray ski mask." Perkins slid a sketch over in front of me.

The sketch looked like one of those Duck Dynasty guys. "The guy had a beard?" I asked, looking at the drawing. "I thought you said he was wearing a ski mask?"

"He was, a ski mask with a beard to keep your face warm—not that anyone in Myrtle Beach would ever need one. I had never seen one before, but apparently they're a new fad. I did a little research. Real popular online. And they sell 'em in lots of retail stores."

"Huh, I've never seen one before, either." I admitted.

"How's *your* thing going?" Perkins asked.

"Just got back from the high school. Spoke with the principal and the coach."

"Focusing on the Davis kid?"

"For now, unless something else comes up."

The door to the lounge opened and a man and woman in their mid-twenties exited in front of Gwen. "Thanks for coming in," she said. "We'll be in touch."

The man shook Gwen's hand and said, "Thank you for everything."

Gwen nodded. "You take care of her, and don't worry, we're going to get this guy."

I smiled one of those pathetic half smiles as the couple walked by me.

When Gwen noticed me standing there she said, "I put the Bowens' financial report on your desk. It's in the folder."

"Thanks, Gwen."

"Where's your partner?" she asked.

"The men's room."

"You ready?" Perkins asked her.

"Yup."

"Where ya headed?" I asked.

"Over to talk to the bartender at the Spanish Galleon," Perkins answered. "You can see the whole parking lot from their front door. The sexual assault victim said she and her boyfriend went there first, and later she saw the bartender out front smoking a cigarette. Maybe he saw something."

"You have fun with that," I said.

I sat down in my chair, leaned back, and opened the file folder to have a look into the Bowens' life.

I don't know what I was expecting to find in their financial records. There was nothing out of the ordinary, just cold hard numbers showing a family living from paycheck to paycheck. A direct deposit into their checking account every two weeks told me one thing: Teachers don't make enough money to put up with little assholes like Jeremy Davis. They surely didn't make enough money to risk being gunned down on the beach on a Sunday morning during a family photo shoot.

What's next? I thought. Might as well head on over to Grand Strand Photography and pay our photographer friend a visit.

I was still looking at the Bowens' paperwork when Lint walked into the room carrying the file folder I had given him earlier. He tossed it on my desk.

"Jesus, Lint, did you take that in the bathroom with you?" I asked.

"Yeah. I like to read when I'm on the shitter. Helps relax things, if ya know what I mean."

"I don't want to know what you mean, and don't do that again."

"What's your problem, Stellar? I didn't wipe my ass with it."

"Just stop talking, Lint. Everything you say just keeps making the image in my head a little worse."

Lint shrugged his shoulders. "Whatever." He started for his desk.

"Take your shit folder with you," I said.

He snatched up the folder and brought it to his desk, sat, and opened it. "Jake, it says here that the Bowens won the photograph session. Was it a raffle or a contest or what?"

"Good question," I said. "We'll head over to the studio in a little while and ask the photographer." I remembered the cell phones. *I wonder if Chavez downloaded the videos yet.*

I picked up the phone and punched number three.

"Chavez."

"Hey, it's Jake. Did you download the video from those cell phones for the Bowen homicide?"

"Sure did. You can bring it up on your computer. It's in a folder marked Bowen Homicide Video."

"Think of that all by yourself, did you?" I asked sarcastically.

"You'd be surprised at the weird and wondrous things that spring from the mind of an electronics genius, my friend."

"I bet. Thanks."

I pulled up the videos and began watching the first one.

"Dammit!" I heard Lint say.

I glanced over. "Find something?"

"Yeah, someone took my last donut right out of the box. What kind of inconsiderate son of a bitch would do that?"

"This kind of inconsiderate son of a bitch," said Captain Merle Stein, chomping on the purloined sinker as he breezed. "You got a problem with that, Lint?"

Lint gulped. "None, sir."

Chapter Ten

The cell phone videos turned up nothing. The only thing the sick bastards recorded was Ellen Bowen lying on her back in the sand, dying. They would have uploaded it to YouTube and had a million hits by now. I decided to tell them they couldn't have their phones back until after the investigation was completed. I also told Chavez to go through those insensitive shithooks' search histories and see if they've ever viewed or downloaded anything they shouldn't have. I know I was being a prick, but I just hated those two douche bags for violating the Bowen family's privacy. I'd make sure the videos had been mysteriously deleted when they finally did get their damn phones back.

When we left the station, I took a right off of Second Avenue onto North Kings Highway. I heard Lint sigh in the passenger seat.

"Were we gonna stop by Sonic for lunch?" he asked.

"Can't you wait until after we talk to the photographer?"

"It's just that I was gonna have that last donut to hold me over, but Stein had to up and steal it."

Again with the donut, I thought.

Lint's stomach rumbled. "See, I'm hungry."

"I can't imagine what's in there making that noise."

"There's nothing in there, that's why it's growling. It's saying, 'Feed me a Footlong Quarter Pound Coney!'" Lint explained in a strange, deep voice that was apparently meant to sound like his stomach.

Grand Strand Photography was located on North Kings Highway in a little strip mall, sandwiched between Direct Auto Insurance and Check 'n Go. To the left of Direct Auto Insurance, conveniently enough, was Nick's Cigar World. We would be making a stop there after we spoke with Alex Caldwell, the photographer.

When we walked in, Caldwell was placing stuffed animals and large wooden blocks on a carpeted table in front of a beach scene backdrop. "Hey," he said when he turned and recognized me. His face instantly adopted a somber look. "How's the investigation going? Poor woman ... those poor kids."

How's the investigation going? Nowadays everyone watches CSI *and* Criminal Minds *and they think they know the lingo.* "The investigation is moving along," I answered.

Alex Caldwell was thirty-nine and just shy of six feet tall. He had a full head of jet-black hair that most men would kill for; he slicked it straight back, tight to his head. He spent way too much time tanning, causing the wrinkles around his eyes that made him look a few years older than he actually was. Today, the outfit he had chosen was a black T-shirt, faded jeans, and a black sport coat. Resting on top of his head was a black porkpie hat. I guess he figured that the hipster hat, along with his soul patch, made him every woman's dream. If not every woman, then at least most of the young moms who brought in their babies for a photo shoot.

"This is Detective Avis Lint," I said.

Caldwell nodded toward Lint. "How's it going, man?" he asked as he continued arranging the oversized building blocks that sat on the beige shag carpeting. He glanced up at a clock on the wall above the door. "Not to rush ya, but I got a shoot at noon,"

"We'll be quick," Lint said.

"Christopher Bowen told us that they had won a free photo shoot," I said. "and that's why they were having their picture taken yesterday at the beach,"

Caldwell smiled. "Yeah, I guess you could say they won it."

"What do you mean?" Lint asked.

I walked over to the counter and looked over the photographs and paperwork scattered around the cash register.

"A few times a year, when things slow down, I send out advertisements for my studio," Caldwell explained. "Folks who fill out the cards and mail them back are entered in a drawing for a free photo shoot."

"And the Bowens won?" Lint asked.

I quietly moved the papers around on the counter. There were bills, notes, and invoices made out in two different styles of handwriting. The sloppy, nearly illegible one was probably Caldwell's; the other, neat and professional, looked more feminine.

"Everyone who enters wins, man," said Caldwell.

I turned back toward Caldwell. "I don't follow, man."

He stopped what he was doing, stood back, and admired his work. "Perfect," he said, and turned in our direction. "I call everyone who sends the cards back and tell them they won. More than half of them make an appointment. It says on the back of the card that the prize is only for one person, so I charge for every extra person. Also, it's only good for one pose. After I show the client all of the photos I've taken, they usually buy extra. Even if they only bring in one kid and take the free photos, I'm only out about a half hour of labor and three dollars' worth of photo stock."

"So it's a scam," Lint said.

Caldwell threw up his hands. "Hey, I don't force them to buy anything. My photos speak for themselves."

Even Lint was a little disgusted. "If they could speak for themselves," he said, "they would probably warn someone."

"Whatever, man. Everyone does it."

"Do you work here alone, Caldwell?" I asked.

"Sure do," he answered.

"Can we take a look at the pictures you took of the Bowen family yesterday morning?" Lint asked. "Maybe you photographed something important without knowing."

"I hadn't taken any yet. I was just setting up my stuff when it happened."

After we finished speaking to Caldwell, Lint said, "We'll be in touch."

As we got to the door Caldwell said. "When you see Mr. Bowen again, tell him … tell him I'm sorry."

"Sorry for what?" I asked. "He was one of your big winners."

Chapter Eleven

At Sonic, I sat at one of the small metal tables across from Lint. I stared in horrific amazement at the way he could eat a footlong hotdog in three bites. Granted, a large percentage of the meal was on his face and the front of his shirt.

I wanted to mention the feminine handwriting that I had noticed at Caldwell's but I knew I had to wait until he swallowed; I didn't want him to join the conversation with a mouthful of food.

I took a bite of my cheeseburger.

He swallowed.

"Hey," I said. "When we were at Caldwell's, I was looking through some of his paperwork while you were questioning him. Some of the handwriting was obviously a woman's."

Lint set down his second dog and took a sip of his soda. "Huh, and he said no one worked with him. Maybe a woman works for him under the table and he was afraid to mention it."

"We're not the IRS," I pointed out. "You wouldn't think he would have lied about it."

"Maybe an illegal."

"Maybe." I took another bite of my burger.

"There's just something about that guy that rubs me the wrong way," Lint commented.

"I know what you mean," I agreed. It was a little irritating to me that Lint and I were working so well together. I was pissed that I had to work with him, period, and now working well with him pissed me off even more. *Maybe it's me and not him*, I thought, but then a big glob of chili dropped from his third hotdog and landed on his tie. He lifted his tie and sucked the chili into his mouth with a god-awful slurping sound. *No, it's him.*

I shoved the last of my fries into my mouth and took a big drink of my 7-UP. "You about ready?"

"Yup," he answered and began picking up his wrappers and empty ketchup packages.

We pulled out of Sonic and took a right onto North Kings Highway. We had only gone about two blocks when Lint looked past me out the driver's side window and said, "I could really go for a Reese's Peanut Butter Cup Sundae."

"For Chrissakes, Lint, you just ate three footlong hotdogs!" I exploded, as I glanced over at Friendly's, but something else caught my eye in the Tiger Mart parking lot, near the pay phone. A white Chevy van sat parked in the first parking spot, right next to the sidewalk.

The traffic light turned red, and I eased into the left hand turn lane. I adjusted my side mirror to look back and see the van. Two men in long, olive green, military-style trench coats stood near the van speaking to each other, their hands in their coat pockets. A third man sat in the van behind the wheel.

One of the men was Caucasian, with blond hair he wore in a short buzz cut. He seemed to be more nervous than the other guy, looking around in every direction as the other man spoke.

The second man was African-America. His head was shaved; he didn't appear to be nervous at all and even laughed a few times.

I looked back up at the traffic light. *A watched pot never boils. And a traffic light never turns green.*

I glanced back into the mirror; both men were now headed toward the building.

The arrow turned green, and I took a left onto Second Avenue North.

"Where are we going?" Lint asked.

"There's something going on at the Tiger Mart."

Lint sat up straight in his seat and his eyes focused on the convenience store.

"I'm going to pull into the Five Guys lot and park," I said. "Two men just went into the front of the building; they're dressed—and acting—suspicious."

"What are they wearing?" Lint asked.

"Long Army coats," I answered.

"Little warm for that."

I pulled into a parking spot directly behind the Tiger Mart. "That's what I thought." I popped the trunk. "I'm going in through the front door; you call for backup and then quietly slip in through the back door."

I jumped from the car and took off running. When I got to the corner of the building, I looked back to see Lint pulling the 12 gauge from the trunk. I rounded the corner.

When I pulled open the door and went in, I was facing the white guy. He was about five feet in front of me. I acted surprised. His revolver was at his side, a .38 caliber snub nose. He brought it up and pointed it at my head. *Yeah, that's right, moron, point the gun at the smallest part of my body.*

"Hold it," he said.

I put up my hands. "Please, don't shoot! I have a wife and seventeen kids, three dogs, a cat, and two birds."

The white guy's face went blank. He blinked stupidly, mentally wrestling with my plea.

The black guy had his sawed-off shotgun leveled at his waist and pointed at the guy behind the checkout counter. He turned toward me. He now seemed a little more nervous than when I had first seen him in the parking lot. "What you say, man? You tryin' to be funny? Darren, keep your gun on him."

"Don't use my real name, Paulie!" the white guy yelled.

I had my hands up. "No, man, I'm not trying to be funny at all." I watched the cashier. He stood behind the counter with his hands up, too, and his eyes kept darting down and to his right and then back at me. I hoped he wasn't looking down at a weapon that he kept there. We didn't need any dead heroes today. "I just came in to grab some baby formula, and some dog food, and some cat food, and so—"

"Shut up, shut up!" Darren hollered. "Or I'll put a bullet through your goddamn head."

I knew it! Paulie turned his shotgun toward me, and the cashier dove for *his* gun.

Beach Shoot

The back door opened, letting in the bright sunlight. Darren turned and squinted.

Paulie caught the worker's movement out of the corner of his eye and spun back, but it was too late, the cashier was firing his pistol without even aiming. Two shots burst up through the counter; one hit the ceiling and the other caught Paulie in the armpit, spinning him around.

My hand shot into my jacket and I yanked my 9mm from its holster.

Paulie fired, and I heard the slug wiz by my ear; a two liter jug of Diet Pepsi exploded behind me.

I fired twice into Paulie's chest, sending him backwards over the counter. I turned my weapon on Darren, he was aiming toward the back door.

It sounded like a cannon when Lint fired the 12 gauge. At that same moment the side of Darren's head exploded and he tumbled back, his lifeless body tangled up in the beef jerky rack.

The van! I remembered, but when I got to the door it was already on its way out of the parking lot. The getaway driver didn't make it far__, a red Ford Taurus broadsided him in the northbound lane.

When I got to the van, the driver was trying to open his door. I stuck my pistol through the open window and pressed the barrel against his temple. "Don't move," I said, "unless you think I might miss from here."

Chapter Twelve

"I'm fine," I said. "It was no big deal." I stood in Tiger Mart parking lot at the corner of North Kings Highway and Second Avenue North. I had called Bree before she had time to see on the news what had happened. "I love you, too. I'll be home in a little while. Bye."

I looked down at Lint. He was sitting on the curb with his ass in some mulch and his back up against a palmetto.

"Is there anyone you want to call?" I asked. He shook his head no.

"Thirty-five years on the job and I've never shot anyone," Lint said. His voice sounded hoarse, disbelieving. "I've only drawn my weapon twice."

"It was a clean shoot, Lint."

"Clean or not, he's still just as dead."

I looked around the parking lot; there were patrol cars everywhere. There was an ambulance near the entrance door of the convenience store and another parked on Second

Avenue. An emergency vehicle from the fire department was parked near where the getaway van had been. The north bound traffic on North Kings Highway was still moving pretty slow. The van, the driver, and the two dead men had been removed from the scene, but it would be another hour or so before everyone else was gone.

I could see Merle through the front window of the store; he was speaking with the cashier.

I ran my fingers through my hair and let out a sigh. "You know what I could really go for?" I asked Lint and held out my hand.

He looked up at me. "What?"

"A Reese's Peanut Butter Cup Sundae."

Lint couldn't help but chuckle. "Not really hungry," he said.

I still had my hand out. "Well, I am. Come on."

He reached up and grabbed my hand, and I pulled him to his feet—no easy task. We walked around the back of the Tiger Mart through the Five Guys parking lot to Friendly's. I motioned toward one of the tables that sat next to a pond. "Go grab that table and I'll bring them over."

When I returned, I was holding a sundae in each hand. I handed one to Lint and took a seat.

We sat on the bench with our backs to the table, staring out over the pond and eating our ice cream in a companionable silence. At length Lint said, "Thanks, Jake."

*****

Beach Shoot

Forty-five minutes later Lint and I were sitting at our desks, he was on the phone with Andrea what's-her-name at the high school, and I was reading through the ballistics report and the CSU findings on the fingerprints and running shoe.

The bullet that was removed from Ellen Bowen didn't match anything in the system, and neither did the three different sets of fingerprints found in the Malibu. One was probably Jeremy Davis', but that was to be expected—after all, it was his vehicle. The running shoe was a Brooks Glycerin 11, men's, size ten and a half, and could be purchased at fourteen different stores in a twenty-mile radius. I printed out a picture of the shoe and placed it in the file folder.

Lint hung up the phone. "How did it go?" I asked.

"It's all set," he answered. "We're meeting Myron Hobbs, that crotchety little janitor, at the school at six tomorrow morning to search lockers."

"I guess we better park in the parking lot and not in the turnaround."

Lint laughed. "Yeah, we wouldn't want to get detention."

Merle's door opened and he stuck his head out. "Will detectives Harry Callahan and Rick Hunter please come in my office?"

Lint and I looked at each other. "I guess he means us," I said.

"Who's Rick Hunter?" Lint asked.

"Just get your asses in here," Merle said.

Lint walked through the door first, and I shut the door behind us. We took a seat in the two chairs facing Merle's desk. It was like being called into the principal's office, only Merle wasn't as pretty as Klaudia Rothstein.

"I just got off the phone with Internal Affairs," Merle said. "It's still under investigation, but their preliminary findings are that today's little drama was a clean shoot. You'll both remain on the street unless otherwise informed."

Lint let out a big sigh. "Thanks, Captain."

"Yeah, thanks Cap'n," I echoed.

"Now get out of here and catch me a killer."

"Yes, sir," we both said in unison.

Lint and I were almost out the door when Merle called out "Oh, and one other thing, did one of you guys call the janitor over at the high school a little weirdo?"

Lint and I exchanged innocent looks. "No," I answered.

"Why would we do that?" Lint asked.

Merle just shrugged and shooed us out of the office with a wave of his hand.

"I'm going to head on home, Jake," Lint said.

"Yeah, me too. I have to go buy running pants tonight."

Chapter Thirteen

I took a left off of Highway Seventeen onto Pine Island Road. There were probably fifty clothing stores within a mile of our house, but here I was fifteen miles away at the Grand Coastal Mall. How did Bree get me there? By promising to buy me dinner at Texas Roadhouse.

Of course, all the way there I was bombarded by questions about the robbery attempt at Tiger Mart. I was also getting an earful of clichéd almost widow's laments, "You could have been killed." "Why didn't you wait for backup?" "Were you wearing a vest?" And the ever-popular "What would I do if anything ever happened to you?" She also managed to slip in a "You should be more careful," which caused me to envision a scenario where I walk into an in-progress robbery attempt and explain to the bad guys that my wife would appreciate it if we were all just a little more careful.

We drove around the parking lot looking for a spot. *It's Monday night, for Chrissakes! Why is everyone at the mall?* My plan was to park so it would be an equal distance from the car to a mall entrance as it was from the car to Texas Roadhouse.

Finally! I noticed two people getting into a black Lincoln at the far end of the row we were in and stepped on it. I sat patiently, three spots away, waiting for the eight-hundred-year-old man and his seven-hundred-year-old bride to back their six hundred-foot-long vehicle out of its resting spot.

Turn the wheel, back up a little, straighten the wheel, pull forward, back up, turn the wheel, put it drive, slam it into reverse. *Come on!*

Mission accomplished! Methuselah pulled away, I eased forward, and a red, four-wheel drive Dodge pickup slid into my spot right in front of me. *Crap!*

The redneck climbed out of his truck, slammed the door, turned his head our way, and smiled. Bree instantly lowered the power window. "Don't do that," I grumbled. "Just put the window up."

"He took our spot!" she said angrily.

As we drove by him he noticed Bree's expression and the shaking of her head and the smile left his face.

"That's telling him," I said.

"He knows what I'm thinking."

"There's plenty of spots," I pointed out. "We'll park somewhere else."

"He did it on purpose."

"Because he's a dick."

"You should have stopped and said something."

"He could be some nut with a gun and shoot me," I joked.

"You're a cop."

"Oh, that's right, so the bullets would probably bounce off the large S on my shirt."

"Whatever."

Strange how she had just told me that I should be more careful, and now she's mad because I didn't do something stupid. She probably wouldn't understand that I felt more comfortable walking into that convenience store with two armed men than I did arguing over a parking space.

We pulled into a spot in the next row and got out. "Remember, we're parked in the purple unicorn section," I said jokingly. It was a line I had used for twenty years that had lost all of its humor.

"Yup," Bree replied unemotionally.

I hit the button on the key fob and locked the doors and we walked toward the mall entrance. I hate going to the mall.

We hadn't made it more than five feet when I heard from behind me, "Hey, asshole, your bitch ever shakes her head at me again, I'll rip off her head and shove it up her ass."

Crap! "Bree," I said calmly, and tossed her the keys. "Get back in the car." She knew from the voice I was using not to question me. She unlocked the doors and climbed in.

When I turned around, the man from the red Dodge was three feet in front of me. *Holy crap, he's big*. He was about four inches taller than me and outweighed me by forty or so pounds. From the look on his face, I was pretty sure that I wasn't going to talk my way out of this one; and if trouble started, I'd better be the one doing all the hitting, because this bruiser would probably only have to hit me once and it would be over.

"Yeah, that bitch *better* get back in the car," he said.

Wow, he does not like Bree. I put up my hands a bit. "Listen, pal, let's just forget this happened and go our separate ways. There's no reason to take it any further."

"Hell yeah, there's a reason! Your wife's a bitch, and you're a little pussy."

Sticks and stones Jake, sticks and stones. " Ya know, pal, it always strikes me as odd that the bigger a guy is and the tougher he pretends to be, the more sensitive he really is."

"Sensitive?" the bruiser asked. "What's that supposed to mean?"

"Well, take my wife for example. She's barely over five feet tall, and she practically has you in tears. Look at you, you're all upset and ready to fight over a harmless little head shake." He just stood there with a stupid look on his face, staring at me. "And you, you're twice the size of me and I'm not scared at all. As a matter of fact, if you even take a swing at me I'm gonna kick you in the balls and break your nose."

He swung.

I ducked.

I shot back up and shoved him in his barrel chest, then kicked his left leg in front of his right leg. The bruiser stumbled backwards landing onto his ass. As soon as he hit the ground, I kicked him in the crotch.

He screamed out in a high-pitched tone that sounded like a cat choking on a banshee.

I leaned over and grabbed his shoulder with my left hand and when he looked up at me I brought my fist down on his nose as hard as I could. When I let go he fell onto his back.

"I warned you," I told him.

When I walked back to the car, Bree got out and whispered, "My hero! But why didn't you just tell him you were a cop?"

"Shh," I said with my finger on my lip. "Because as it is he won't tell anyone about the guy who kicked his ass, but if he knew I was a cop, then the headline in tomorrow's paper would read, PSYCHO COP BEATS MAN OVER PARKING SPOT.

Bree looked back as the humbled bruiser was getting to his feet, she gave him an over-exaggerated head shake and we went in to buy a few pairs of running pants that she really didn't need.

Chapter Fourteen

I followed Bree through the maze of clothing racks in store after store. She hadn't purchased any running pants as of yet, but she did buy two *tops*. Why she can't just call them shirts I'll never know. She also bought a pair of jeans from a store where the denim was obviously spun from some rare form of faded blue gold. They couldn't have been made from the same material as mine because they cost three times as much. She also tried on, but didn't buy, two pairs of magical stretch pants. I know they were magical because when a woman who is just over five feet tall and only weighs one hundred and twenty pounds tries them on, she instantly becomes fat and large pockets of cellulite appear on the backs of her legs where no cellulite previously was. After we left that store it dawned on me that maybe the stretch pants weren't magical: Maybe it was the mirror.

"Can I help you find anything today?" a teenaged salesgirl at Old Navy asked.

"Yes," I answered quickly. "Where is the exit?"

Bree swung her hand back but I dodged it. Quick on my feet. "No thank you," Bree replied. "Just looking."

I wished we were *just looking*. *Just looking* costs a lot less that *just buying*. But hey, it ain't my money. If it was, we would be at Kmart.

Bree held up a top in front of her. "Do you like this?"

Before I even had a chance to answer the same salesgirl remarked, "Oh, I like that! It'll go great with your eyes."

Someone's getting paid on commission, I thought. Obviously, this young girl knows clothes__, after all, she's been wearing them her whole life. And besides, they wouldn't just give *anyone* a headset and two-way radio. Those tools are reserved only for the elite, like the Secret Service and seventeen-year-old girls who work at Old Navy.

"I'm going to try this on," Bree informed me, and made her way toward the dressing rooms.

"I'll be here." I leaned against a rack of capris that had been marked down 60 percent and pulled out my cell phone. No one had texted me about the case. I wondered how Lint was doing. I wondered why I was wondering that.

Wife number three, Eunice, had left four years ago, so I knew he was probably sitting home all by himself, thinking about what had happened earlier in the day.

I thought about calling him, but I needed an excuse. I didn't want him to know I was calling to see how he was.

I searched through my contacts. *I must have his number in here somewhere. There it is.* I dialed.

"Hello," Lint answered.

"Hey, it's Jake."

His voice brightened up a little bit. "Hey, Jake! What's up?"

"You said six o'clock tomorrow morning, right?" I asked.

"Yeah, that's right six o'clock."

"Did you want to meet me there or at the station?"

"Um … meet me at the station and we'll ride over together."

"Okay … How's everything going?"

"Good, ya know. Just watching a little TV. You want to come over and have a drink, Jake?"

Crap! "Jeez, Lint, I would, but Bree and I are at the mall and we're going to go over to the Texas Roadhouse for dinner after."

"That sounds great!" Lint remarked. "I'll get dressed and meet you guys there. What, about forty-five minutes sound good?"

"Uh … yeah … that sounds good."

"See ya then," he said and hung up.

The dressing room door opened just a crack and Bree peeked out. When she saw me she pushed it the rest of the way open. "How's this look?"

"Great," I replied. "Goes real good with your eyes."

"Funny," she said and closed the door.

*****

I didn't say much on the way back to the car. I placed the bags in the car and shut the trunk. I made a point to look around and make sure the bruiser with the broken schnozz hadn't waited for us to come out.

"We walking over to the restaurant?" Bree asked.

"Mmm-hmm," I replied.

She took my hand as we walked. "Something wrong?"

"Avis Lint is joining us for dinner."

"Okay … Why? This is unusual."

"I called him to see how he was doing while you were in the dressing room and he kind of invited himself."

"You called him to see how he was doing?"

"Yeah."

Bree pulled me in closer and rested her head against my arm. "Awe, you are a good friend."

"He's not my friend."

Chapter Fifteen

I rolled over in bed, opened my eyes, and clasped my fingers together behind my head. My first thought that morning was, how the hell did Lint talk us into eating at Cracker Barrel instead of Texas Roadhouse?

The alarm hadn't gone off, so it wasn't four-thirty yet. I lifted my head and looked at the clock, 4:26. *I should probably get up now and turn off the alarm so it doesn't wake up Bree.* Today was her day off, every other Tuesday. Must be nice; weekend off, go back to work for one day, and have another day off.

I got out of bed, flipped off the alarm, and made my way down the hall to make a cup of coffee. What would it be, blueberry, hazelnut, pumpkin spice? I went with the blueberry.

Halfway down the hall, I stopped at our bedroom door. Bree was turning over. "You awake?" I whispered.

"Yup."

"Want a cup of coffee?"

"Sure."

I returned to the Keurig and also chose blueberry for her. I returned to the bedroom and sat the cup on the nightstand. "Here ya go."

"Thanks."

"Love you."

"I love you, too."

After my shower I went to the living room and turned on the Weather Channel, then walked out to the driveway to grab the newspaper. I never told anyone, but there wasn't a morning that I walked out to get the paper that I didn't think of my old partner, Sam Chandler, Officer Gary Finder, or Helen Gere. I wondered if that was normal, I wondered if I should talk to someone about it.

When I went back inside, Bree was walking into the kitchen. "Want me to make you something for breakfast?" she asked.

"No, that's okay; I was just going to throw a Pop-Tart in the toaster."

Bree opened the cupboard and grabbed a box of the strawberry, unfrosted; she knew what I liked. She opened the package and placed the two glorious rectangles in the toaster. She stood there for about ten seconds and then reached over and turned the dial all the way up. "We need a new toaster," she claimed.

I unfolded the paper. "There's nothing wrong with the toaster," I argued.

"It takes forever to toast anything. You have to turn the dial all the way up to get it hot enough."

"That dial is a timer, not a heat setting."

"Either way, I have to turn it all the way to high."

Beach Shoot

I turned the page and took a sip of my coffee. "Maybe you should turn it up to eleven. I hear that works for amps."

She didn't get it.

When I glanced over, she was leaving the room. "Where ya going?" I asked.

"Putting some towels in the washing machine," she answered.

She had already forgotten about the Pop-Tarts. If those were *her* Pop-Tarts and I wasn't here to pop them up, then the entire house would smell like burnt toaster pastries when I got home from work tonight. I walked over, got a plate, and popped them up manually.

I was halfway through the second Pop-Tart when she ran back into the room.

"Forget something?" I asked.

"Shut up," she said, and returned to the laundry room.

Chapter Sixteen

I walked into the station at five-forty; Lint was at his desk with an open folder and a half-eaten box of Krispy Kremes. "Mornin', partner," he called out, raising his donut into the air. "Care for a glazed donut?"

"No thank you. Bree made me a big breakfast this morning," I lied.

"More for me."

Yes there is. "You ready to head over to the school?"

"Ready when you are."

"Let's go."

We met three patrol cars at the school. We all parked in the circle near the flagpole, Myron would not like this.

"Good morning, Myron," Lint said as we walked through the doors.

The old sentry was not at her post. Probably out on the highway pecking at roadkill.

Myron just said, "Yeah," and removed a key from his belt.

I opened the file folder I had brought with me and handed out a picture of the running shoe to each of the six uniforms. "We're looking for this type of shoe, not necessarily in this color, a size ten and a half."

Myron was already halfway down the hall, unlocking lockers and opening them. The eight of us searched through the lockers one by one for the next forty-five minutes, finding four pairs of men's, Brooks Glycerin 11s. Two pairs were a size nine, one pair was a size nine and a half, and the fourth was a seven and a half. We did not find the shoe we were looking for. However, we did find thirteen bags of marijuana, two switch-blades, several knives, twenty bottles of prescription medication, and one very large clear freezer bag of unidentified pills. A lot of notes would be going home today.

Lint and I walked to the office with a cardboard box filled with the confiscated material and a list with each locker number coinciding with its contraband.

"Myron!" I hollered as I looked down the hall toward Coach Pawlak's office.

"Yeah?" he yelled back.

I quickly read down through the search warrant. "Could you come here for a second?"

Lint chuckled when he figured out what was next.

"What's up?" Myron asked when he reached us.

"Are there any lockers in Coach Pawlak's office?" I asked.

"Well, yeah … there's a few on the wall behind his desk."

"Can you open his door for me, please?"

"There's no student lockers in there," Myron informed me.

"The search warrant doesn't limit us to student lockers."

"I'll have to ask," Myron said. "I don't know if I'm supposed to open a faculty member's door."

"I'll just kick it in," Lint said, and started toward the door.

"No, no, wait, I'll get it," Myron said nervously, and led the way to the coach's door.

We went inside. Myron flipped on the lights, and then opened each locker. Taped to the inside of the last locker door was a color 5x7 photograph of little Jenna. She was sporting her signature ponytail, a smile, a pair of dark blue thong panties with the Superman logo, and that's about it.

"Stevie and Jenna, sitting in a tree," Lint sang out.

"What's going on here?" came a gruff voice behind us. We turned to see Coach Pawlak. I swung open the locker door so he could see what we had found.

"She's seventeen … she's seventeen," Pawlak blurted out.

"Her being seventeen gives you the right to be a piece of shit?" Lint asked.

"Detective Lint, will you please read Mr. Pawlak his rights and place him under arrest?" I glared at Pawlak. "You better get used to the *Mr.* part, because no one will ever call you coach again."

"But she's seventeen," he repeated.

"Stevie, you and I both know that doesn't matter," I said. "You're a teacher, she's a student ... it's a felony."

Lint closed the cuffs around Pawlak's wrists slow enough for him to hear each click, and then he put his mouth right next to his ear. "If she really loves you, Steverino, maybe she'll still be waiting for you when you get out."

Chapter Seventeen

Arresting Steve Pawlak was going to create a lot of extra paperwork, but it was worth it. We didn't turn up any evidence in the Bowen investigation, but I still felt pretty good about the day so far. We were back at the station by seven-thirty.

Merle's door opened and he walked over to my desk. "Pawlak lawyered up," he said. "You'll have to hold off on questioning him."

I grinned. "That's fine. I've already put in a call to Child Protective Services. They'll want to talk to the girl and her family before I do."

"How's it going with Lint?" Merle asked quietly.

"Pretty good, actually."

"Perkins and Lawrence are at the hospital; another young woman was attacked early this morning."

"God dammit. She okay?"

"No. She was walking back to the Ocean Bay Club alone. The guy grabbed her in the parking garage and dragged her down to the beach. He raped her."

"They think it's the same guy?" I asked.

"I haven't heard back from them yet."

"If it is, he's pretty brave," I pointed out. "Two attacks in two nights."

"Yeah," Merle agreed. "We're going to have to speak to the press."

"Let Lint do it," I said sarcastically.

"Yeah, right," Merle said and went back toward his office. "I got a lot of phone calls to make."

Dill Perkins and Gwen Lawrence walked through the door. I looked over but waited for one of them to speak first.

"Did you hear?" Perkins asked.

"Yeah," I answered.

"Two in two nights," Gwen said numbly.

"*This* girl wasn't as lucky as the first," Dill said. "He beat her up pretty bad."

"Yeah, I heard. Same guy?" I asked.

Dill shook his head yes. "She described the same hat, the one with a beard."

"The Beardo," Lint said matter-of-factly.

We all looked over. "What?" Gwen said.

"Those hats with the beards, they call them Beardos."

"Are ya shittin' me?" I asked.

"Nope," Lint answered. "It's the Beardo."

I returned my attention to Perkins and Gwen. "Any description?"

"She said she couldn't see his whole face, of course, but enough to see that he was white." Gwen pulled her notepad from her back pocket and flipped it open. "Said he was about six feet tall and weighed about two hundred pounds. Walked with a slight limp."

"She fought back the entire time," Perkins added. "We got tissue samples from under the fingernails on both hands, and judging from the amount of tissue, he will have some pretty obvious injuries to his back and thighs."

"That, along with the bodily fluids that were collected. If he's in the system, we got him." Gwen said optimistically.

"Let's hope he is," I said.

Pat Murray walked into the room. "Jake," he said, "I thought you might want to know, we had a 911 call come in from Grand Strand Photography. Two minutes later another call came in from a guy who said he owned the place and that it was a false alarm."

"Thanks, Pat," I said. I looked over toward Lint, and he was already dragging his bulk across the room.

"There's a unit on its way over now," Pat added as I got to the door.

*****

When Lint and I arrived at Grand Strand Photography, we observed a squad car already in the parking lot. I recognized Officer Don Quinn trying to calm a clearly agitated Alex Caldwell, standing at the store's entrance with a broom in his hand.

We came to a stop and climbed out of the vehicle.

"Everything's fine, everything's fine," Caldwell was saying, fidgeting nervously with the broom. He had a forced smile across his face that was supposed to convince us that everything was indeed fine, but with his demeanor—the glass smashed out of the front door__, I wasn't buying it.

Lint and I nodded at Quinn. "What happened here, Caldwell?" I asked. I saw traces of blood on the doorjamb and visually inspected Caldwell's arms and hands for injuries but saw none.

"Detective Stellar, I was just explaining to this officer that I had a little mishap and broke my door."

"We received a 911 call," Lint said.

"Yes," Caldwell explained. "That was a mistake. A woman walking by thought that something was wrong and called the police. I called back immediately and told them it was a false alarm."

"Sir, we have to come out and make sure everything is okay whether you call back or not," Officer Quinn explained.

"Well now that you've seen that everything is fine, you can go and let me get this cleaned up." Caldwell pulled his wallet from his hip pocket. "Here, let me buy you gentlemen a cup of coffee for your trouble."

Lint glanced over at me with a raised eyebrow. "Mr. Caldwell, why don't you let us come in and have a look around."

"No, that's not necessary."

Beach Shoot

It was obvious he didn't want us in that building, and the closer we got the more anxious he became. "Mr. Caldwell, is there someone in the building that's forcing you to tell us to leave?" I asked. "Just say no, if there is."

Caldwell looked confused.

Lint cocked his head toward the door, pretending that something inside had caught his attention. "Jake, did you hear that?" he asked.

"I sure did. Mr. Caldwell, could you please step aside so we can secure the building?"

Caldwell leaned his broom up against the stuccoed wall and stepped aside in defeat.

Officer Quinn drew his weapon and entered the studio first, followed by me, and then Lint. The broken glass crunched beneath our feet as we went in.

The cash register had been knocked off the counter, so I stepped over it and looked around the room. Paperwork and photographs were strewn about. A four-foot-tall file cabinet to my left had been pushed over; all of the drawers were pulled out and the contents had been scattered around the room. The props that Caldwell had so carefully positioned the day before had been shoved off their stand onto the floor.

Lint opened a door near where the file cabinet sprawled; it led to a bathroom. Quinn opened another door behind the counter. It was an office, and it was in about the same shape as the studio.

I looked back. Caldwell was standing in the doorway, his broom once again in his hand. "I think you're going to need more than a broom," I pointed out. Caldwell said nothing.

"So, after your little mishap with the door, I'm guessing a small tornado came through?" Lint asked. Quinn quietly chuckled.

"What happened here, Caldwell?" I demanded.

He let out a sigh. "Someone broke in."

"Obviously," Lint said.

"You didn't think you should report this?" Quinn asked.

"I uh … I looked around and nothing was missing," Caldwell answered.

Lint rubbed his furrowed brow. "How can you tell?"

"Why don't you tell us what's really going on here," I said.

"I don't know what you mean," Caldwell protested. "Nothing's going on. I'm the victim here. Someone broke into my studio, and you're talking to me like I'm the criminal!"

Lint put up his hand. "Calm down. No one is accusing you of anything."

"It's just a little strange that you had a breakin and you don't want us involved," I added.

Quinn pulled his notepad from his belt. "Why don't you tell me exactly what happened, Mr. Caldwell and we'll go from there."

Caldwell let out another loud sigh. "Fine," he said, and began telling Officer Quinn what he found when he arrived.

Lint and I looked around for a little while, trying not to disturb anything. As we made our way back to the door I turned to Quinn and said, "I'll call in CSU to check for prints and take a few photographs. Don't let Mr. Caldwell touch anything."

"You still suspect me, don't you?" I didn't want you involved because I have several appointments today."

Lint smiled. "Let me guess; more of your lucky contest winners."

"You'll probably want to cancel those appointments," I added.

When Lint and I got back in the car, he turned to me and said, "He's got something to do with the Bowen homicide."

"I know. This was no coincidence. Someone was looking for something."

"We have to find out who he has working for him that he doesn't want us to know about."

"I wish we had enough to get a warrant for his phone records," I said.

Lint reached inside his jacket pocket and pulled out a cell phone. "Yeah, I don't think we'll need a warrant."

"Jesus! Did you take his phone?"

"I don't know that it's *his* phone, but I know it's *a* phone, found at the scene of a break-in that we're investigating. But here," he said, tossing me the cell, "you can give it back if you want."

I shook my head and opened the phone. "Get out a pencil and write down these numbers," I grumbled as I quickly went through the call log.

After I had read off four or five of the most called numbers in Caldwell's recent call history, I had Lint take the cell phone back inside and inconspicuously drop it on the floor somewhere.

As we pulled out of the parking lot I said, "If something comes of this, we'll have to explain where we got these phone numbers."

"I'm sure we'll think of something. After all, we're a couple of bright guys."

Chapter Eighteen

We ran all five of the phone numbers from Alex Caldwell's cell phone; they were all cell numbers. Nancy Ray was fifty-five years old and lived on Wood Hollow Lane in Little River. Marita Perry was eighty-four and lived in Carolina Forrest on Southgate Parkway. One of the numbers belonged to Capital One and another to Carolina Bank. The number that seemed out of place was for a Nicole Irvine, a senior at North Myrtle Beach High School. She was eighteen, and lived on Ash Street, right here in North Myrtle Beach.

Sure, maybe an eighteen-year-old girl would call a portrait studio to make an appointment to have her picture taken. After all, she was a senior, and maybe it was for senior portraits. But why would she call ten times in the last two weeks, and why would Caldwell call her eight times over the same period?

We decided to take a ride back over to the high school and ask a few questions about Miss Irvine.

"Thank you for seeing us again on such short notice, Klaudia," I said as we walked into her office. I still had to bite my tongue, to keep from laughing every time I said that frumpy name, straight out of some nineteenth century romance novel.

"It's the least I could do," she answered. "Please have a seat."

Lint and I sat in the same chairs as the day before. "We were wondering if you could tell us about a young woman who's a senior here, Nicole Irvine."

"Oh, yes, Nikki. I know her very well." Klaudia paused for a second. "She's a good girl; she babysits for my husband and me. She lives right around the corner from us. This doesn't have anything to do with Emily's murder, does it?"

"Her name has just come up a few times in our investigation," I lied. "and we are just following up."

"Klaudia, do you know if Nikki has a part-time job, after school maybe?" Lint asked.

Klaudia thought for a second. "Yes, she does. I'm not sure of the name of the place. It's at a photography studio, right here in town. I think she works a few days after school, maybe even Saturday afternoons."

Lint glanced over at me, then back at Klaudia.

"Could it be Grand Strand Photography?" I asked.

"It could be; I don't know, there are so many of them," she answered.

"Could you check and see if she is in school today?" Lint asked.

Klaudia tapped a few keys on her computer. "No, she's not. As a matter of fact, she's been out all week. Strange. I hope nothing is wrong."

I stood, and Lint followed suit. "Thank you, Klaudia," I said, and we started out the door. After Lint had left the room, I stopped and turned back. "Does Nikki have a boyfriend that you know of?"

Klaudia smiled and nodded yes. "Paul Neil. He's also a senior here. I think they've been dating, since, like ninth grade. Paul's going into the Air Force after graduation."

"Can you give us Paul's address, please?"

"I can," she said, hit a few more keys, wrote the address down on a yellow Post-it note and handed it to me.

"Thanks. And Klaudia, can you please not mention to anyone that we asked about Nikki or Paul?"

She nodded. "You have my word. And Detective?"

"Yes?"

"You'll solve Emily's murder, won't you? And look into Nikki's absence from school?"

"You have *my* word Klaudia."

*****

"Merle, the name Nicole Irvine has come up a few times in our investigation of the Bowen homicide," I lied, for the second time. Hey, the lie worked on Klaudia Rothstein; who knows, maybe Merle wouldn't ask any questions either. "We think she may work part-time at Alex Caldwell's studio."

"The thing is," Lint cut in, "Caldwell told us that he had no employees and worked alone."

"She probably works under the table," Merle pointed out.

"That's what we figured," I agreed. "She hasn't been in school since the shooting, and we were going to head over to her address and ask her a few questions."

"Ooo*okay*," Merle said slowly. "Why are you telling me this? Is she a minor?"

"No," Lint responded. "She's eighteen. We just wanted to give you a heads up."

"Yeah, go ahead then." We were almost out the door when Merle said, "How did her name keep coming up?"

"Excuse me?" I asked.

"Nicole Irvine. You said her name came up a few times."

"That's right," Lint said.

"*How* did it come up?" Merle pressed. "In what context?"

Lint looked at me with an exaggerated look of confusion. "How did her name come up, Jake?" he said.

"Um … I don't really recall. I would have to look in my notes," I said, clumsily sidestepping the truth.

Now Merle looked confused, too. "Just go," he said, and shooed us out the door with a trademark wave of his hand.

Chapter Nineteen

We drove to the Irvine residence at 108 Ash Street and knocked on the door. There were no cars in the driveway, and no one answered the door. We wondered if Nicole was home by herself and thought it best not to open the door to two strange men, so Lint called through the door that we were detectives from the North Myrtle Beach Police Department. As proof, we held up our shields in front of the peephole.

I pulled out my cell phone. Luckily, I had saved Nicole's number in my contacts, so I dialed it and we listened. We didn't hear a cell phone ringing inside the home, and no one answered, so I left a message. "Nicole Irvine, this is Detective Jake Stellar with the North Myrtle Beach Police Department. We were wondering if you could come down to the station sometime today and answer a few questions for us regarding your employment at Grand Strand Photography. You're not in any trouble. We just want to ask you a few questions."

I left my cell number so she could call me back, then we looked up the Irvine's landline number and left the same message on their answering machine.

As we walked back to the car, Lint asked, "Are you hungry? I'm hungry."

"I could eat," I answered.

Lint tried to talk me into Wendy's but I figured it was my turn to choose, so I went with Duffy Street Seafood Shack, over on Main Street. I chose Duffy's partly because I really liked the food, but also because it was located near where both sexual assaults had occurred. I wanted to sit outside and eat at one of the picnic tables and people-watch.

"Can't we sit inside?" Lint whined. "I want to scarf some peanuts and throw the shells on the floor."

"What are you, six? It's a beautiful day out. We're sitting outside."

Lint sighed. "Fine."

I ordered a Fish Po' Boy platter that came with hush puppies, fries, and coleslaw. I also got a soda. Lint ordered smoked BBQ ribs, fish, corn, and crab soup, and Buffalo shrimp for an appetizer. *A forty dollar lunch,* I thought, as I quickly added it up in my head, *and he's going to want to split the check.*

I chose the picnic table that sat closest to Bargain World. We took our seats, with me facing South Ocean Boulevard.

As we waited for our food to arrive, we discussed Perkins' and Gwen's sexual assault case. I filled Lint in on what I knew about it and pointed out the parking lot directly behind him where the first woman was abducted.

Beach Shoot

"So the suspect limps, and both attacks took place within a three block area," Lint said. "Sounds like the guy might not have a vehicle and doesn't want to walk very far."

"Yeah, that's what I was thinking." It bugged me that we were on the same page. I liked Lint a lot better when I hated him.

"A lazy serial rapist," Lint said. "I wonder how common that is."

"Or maybe he's in too much pain to walk very far."

"But if you don't own a car and can't walk too far, why would you commit crimes in your own neighborhood where someone might recognize you?"

"He would have to take a bus or a cab," I pointed out.

"Too late for a bus," Lint said.

Lint's appetizer arrived, and his face lit up like Augustus Gloop seeing the river of chocolate for the first time. He pushed the plate to the center of the table. "Have some," he said.

I might as well, I thought. *I'll be paying for half of them anyway.*

Lint's soup came shortly after, then our food, and the sassy waitress refilled our glasses. "Perkins said they spoke with the bartender at the Spanish Galleon because the victim remembered seeing him outside shortly before she was attacked," I remarked, "but he didn't remember seeing anyone, or anything unusual. What is unusual is the ski mask with a beard. What did you say it was called?"

"The Beardo," Lint replied. You know, you can buy those hats with beards anywhere now, and a lot of people make them."

"Make them?"

"Yeah, they're just made out of yarn. People knit or crochet them, or whatever they do, and sell them at all of the area flea markets and farmers markets. I've got one somewhere at my house. Bought it just for kicks. Always gets a big laugh."

I bet. I took a bite of my sandwich. "You're lucky you don't walk with a limp."

Lint chuckled. "Maybe they've got them at Bargain World. We could go see."

"Yeah, let's."

After we finished lunch, we walked next door to the Bargain World. I wanted to see one of these ridiculous hats everyone seemed to know about but me.

The kid behind the counter was no kid. He was probably thirty-five, but he desperately wanted to be seventeen. He looked a little bit like Shaggy from the Scooby-Doo cartoons. He wore a tie-dyed T-shirt and a pair of baggy shorts that ended just above his ankles. Every time I saw a young man in a pair of those shorts, I couldn't help but wonder *why*. Who was the genius that saw a market for shorts that were as long as regular pants? If I invented a short-sleeve shirt with sleeves that went all the way to your wrists, would it be a big hit? Who knows, maybe someday I'll invent a thong that covers your entire ass and make a fortune.

"Excuse me," I said. "I'm looking for one of those knit hats that have a beard attached to them."

He grinned and nodded his head, looking eerily like a giant Shaggy Bobblehead. "Yo, dude, you're talking about the Beardo. Love those, man."

"Do you carry them here, *dude*?" Lint asked impatiently.

"Sure do. They're right over on the back wall, next to all the other hats."

"Thanks, dude," I said, and the two of us made our way to the back of the store.

"Here they are," Lint said, pulling one off the rack and slipping it over his head. "How do I look?"

"Like a rapist," I responded. I grabbed one and inspected it. "Twenty-five bucks?"

"Yeah. You gonna get one?"

"No. Didn't you hear me? Twenty-five bucks. I just wanted to see what they were."

"No Beardo for the cheapo," Lint remarked.

"Funny." I headed for the door.

As we walked past the counter, Shaggy asked, "Didn't see anything you like?"

"Nope," I responded.

Just as we got back to the car my cell phone rang, it was the Irvine's land line. "Detective Stellar," I answered.

"Hello, Detective, this is Mark Irvine, Nicole's father."

"Yes, Mr. Irvine. We were wondering if your daughter could come down to the station this afternoon and answer some questions about her employer, Alex Caldwell."

"She doesn't work there anymore."

"We would still like her to come in."

"Is this about the shooting Sunday?"

"Mr. Irvine, this is something I would rather not discuss on the phone. We can send a car for your daughter, if that would be more convenient."

"No, no, I'll bring her. Should we have a lawyer present?"

"That's up to you, sir. If you feel your daughter needs a lawyer, she has every right to have one present."

"What time should we come over?"

I looked at my watch. "Is three-thirty good for you?"

"We'll see you then, Detective."

Chapter Twenty

When Mark Irvine and his daughter Nicole walked into the police station, they were alone, no attorney. Whenever you tell someone they can bring a lawyer if they feel they need one, they rarely do. Not bringing representation is their way of proving to you that they have nothing to hide and have done nothing wrong. It's just human nature to try so hard to prove your innocence, even when you haven't done anything.

We took them into the interrogation room instead of the lounge, I figured if she had something to tell us, it would come out a little easier if she was scared. I chose to go in alone, without Lint, to avoid making Mark Irvine feel as though it was two against one.

Nicole sat directly across from me, her father to her right. Mark sold insurance and had just come home from the office when he got my message. He was still in his suit and tie.

Nicole was a beautiful young woman with long brown hair, tinted reddish at the tips. She had dark skin, and eyes so blue they put Frank Sinatra's and Paul Newman's celebrated peepers to shame. She couldn't have been more than five feet tall and she probably weighed a hundred pounds soaking wet.

I set the file folder I was carrying on the table and sat down. "Can I get either one of you something to drink?" I asked.

"No, thank you," Mark said. Nicole just shook her head no.

"Nicole, your father has told me that you no longer work for Mr. Caldwell at his studio."

She stared at the tabletop, picking her fingernails. "No, I quit last Wednesday," she responded, her voice just above a whisper.

"Why did you quit?"

"It wasn't working out with school. It didn't leave me much time for homework."

"I'm sure you've heard that Emily Bowen, a teacher at your school, was murdered Sunday morning."

She nodded her head yes. A tear hit the back of her hand, and she wiped her eye.

"Mrs. Rothstein told us that Mrs. Bowen was a great teacher and that everyone liked her. Is that true, Nicole?"

She shook her head yes again. "I liked her a lot."

"Nikki gets along well with all of her teachers__, she's a straight A student," her father said, beaming.

I reached out and put my hand on hers. "Nikki, I know this is hard for you, but if there is anything that you can tell us that will help us in our investigation, now is the time to tell me."

Mark showed real concern for the first time during the interview and leaned in close to his daughter. He put his hand on her back. "Nikki, you can tell the detective anything."

"I don't know anything," she answered.

I opened the folder. I had placed a picture of Emily Bowen's lifeless body on top of the paperwork purposely. Nicole glanced over and then quickly away. I took out a piece of paper with some of my notes and closed the folder. Another tear hit the table. "You have a boyfriend named Paul Neil," I said.

"Yes," she responded.

"Were you with him Saturday night or Sunday morning?"

"I was with him at a party Saturday night. They dropped me off between twelve and twelve-thirty."

"They?" I asked.

"Paul and Jeremy."

"Jeremy Davis?"

"Yes."

"And do you know where Paul and Jeremy went after they dropped you off?"

"Paul dropped Jeremy off at his house, and then Paul walked home."

"Paul left his car at Jeremy's house?" I asked.

"No. Paul was driving Jeremy's car. Jeremy was really drunk."

I turned to Mark. "Did you hear Nicole come in?"

"Yes, it was around the time she said it was," he answered.

"Were you home the morning of the shooting?" I asked.

Mark thought for a second. "No, as a matter of fact, the three of us went to breakfast that morning."

I removed the photograph of the running shoe from the folder. "Nikki, do you know if Paul or Jeremy owns a pair of sneakers like this?"

She glanced at the picture and shook her head no.

I placed the photo back in the folder and stood up. I reached out to shake Mark's hand. "Thank you very much for coming in," I said.

I held the door open for both of them and when Nicole had walked a little further ahead, Mark turned back toward me. "You don't think Paul or Jeremy had anything to do with that woman being murdered, do you?"

"At this point we're looking into everything, Mr. Irvine. Once again, thanks for coming in, and if you or Nicole think of anything, anything at all, please give me a call."

After they left, I rejoined Lint in the squad room. He leaned back in his chair and drummed his fat fingers on his whiskey keg of a belly. "How did it go in there?" he asked.

"Nicole and her boyfriend, Paul, were at the same party as Jeremy Davis. Paul gave them both rides home in Jeremy's car. According to her, Paul left the car at the Davis house and walked home."

"So, the Davis boy left that part out of his story," Lint commented.

"Exactly, which means we don't even know if Jeremy's car *was* stolen from the house. It may never have been there in the first place."

"What's next?"

"We'll bring the boyfriend in tomorrow and see what he has to say." I opened my desk drawer, pulled out my weapon, and clipped it on my belt. "I'm going to head on home."

"Yeah, I'm gonna finish up some paperwork and then get out of here myself."

"See ya tomorrow."

"Yup."

Chapter Twenty-One

When I left the station, I called Bree to ask her if she had started dinner yet. She wasn't even home. She and a friend had spent the day shopping and were now at Barefoot Landing.

"Why don't you meet us *here* for dinner?" Bree suggested.

I really had my heart set on a nice juicy steak, cooked on my own grill, in my own back yard. "I don't want to have dinner with you and a friend. I won't have anyone to talk to. I hate being the third wheel." *Three excuses in one sentence; I'm getting good at this.*

"She's going to call Luca and have him meet us here, too. He's at the gym right now," Bree said.

Of course he's at the gym. Ugh. Luca Trentinni: bodybuilder, part-time karate instructor, and banker. Put all those things together, along with his goodfella-ish name, and he sounds like he should be the star of *Godfather IV: The Octagon.*

Bree and Aida have tried to pair the two of us up for about three years now. It hasn't worked in the past, and it's not going to work now. I don't need another friend, and I don't want to spend my evening with a muscle-bound ninja.

"I would rather not. Why don't you guys grab dinner and I'll make something for myself," I said. I put on my blinker to inform the asshole that was tailgating me that I was about to make a right into BI-LO to purchase a slab of Certified Angus goodness.

Bree kept at it. "Come on, it'll be fun."

"Really, Bree? He's a bodybuilding ninja. Have you never met me? I don't want to have dinner with a ninja any more than I want to have dinner with a Jedi, a Vulcan, a wizard, or a Time Lord. And do you remember the last time we went to dinner with them? He ordered a $200 bottle of wine and then we split the check. I don't even drink wine!"

"Well, she already called him and he's meeting us here, so get in the shower, get dressed and get over here."

Wow! That quickly turned from a suggestion into an order.

"I better be getting steak."

She hung up the phone, and I made a U-turn in the BI-LO parking lot.

*****

While I showered, I thought about T-Bonz; they have good steak. While I shaved, I got thinking about Greg Norman's; the steak there is pretty good. As I climbed back into my truck, I remembered the steak I had once ordered at Castano's; that was *really* good.

As I drove up Twenty-Fifth Avenue toward North Kings Highway, I called Bree. "Where am I meeting you?"

"Meet us at Hiro," Bree answered.

"Good one," I said. "Seriously, where am I meeting you?"

"Hiro," she repeated, this time a little quieter.

"What the hell, Bree? Japanese?" *Am I on a hidden camera show, because this can't be happening.*

"Luca was in the mood for sushi. He said this place is really good."

"Oh, what a surprise, the ninja was in the mood for sushi. Thank God he doesn't think he's a Klingon or we would be eating a big dish of blood pie for dinner."

Bree whispered into the phone. "Only a nerd would know that a Klinger eats blood pie."

"Yeah, well, this nerd detective was in the mood for steak," I informed her. "And it's Klingon, not Klinger. Klinger was on M*A*S*H."

"I'm sure they have steak at Hiro."

"I didn't want steak *teriyaki*, I wanted just plain old regular steak." I hung up my phone just about the time I pulled into the parking lot. The three of them were standing near the entrance. I was wearing my gun. I could just shoot myself right here in the parking lot. Luca smiled and waved, I wondered if he liked me, or if he just pretended better than I did. I bet if I shot myself, that douche would show up at my funeral and tell everyone that we were really good friends. *Crap!* He'd better die first__, then I'll show up at *his* funeral and tell everyone that I always thought he was a douche.

I climbed out of my truck and forced a smile. The only Japanese I knew was "*Domo Arigato,* Mr. Roboto," so I just went with, "Hey, Luca, long time, no see." He fell for the act and shook my hand. Of course, just to show how strong he was, he had to squeeze my hand about three times harder than a normal human being.

Being September, the tourist off-season, there was no wait to be seated. Maybe there was no wait because everyone else was at a *good* restaurant, having steak. I made the mistake of sitting first, and Luca sat down to my left. *Dammit, I wanted him across from me. He's too close.* I hated the deadly combination of sweat and cheap, musky cologne that made my eyes water. I hated the way he rubbed the Kirk Douglas cleft in his chin to call attention to it. I hated the way he constantly flexed his arm and pectoral muscles. I hated the air the insufferable prick breathed.

After looking at our menus for a few minutes, Luca ordered the sushi regular. Aida and Bree both ordered the chicken teriyaki. I ordered the *steak* teriyaki. *Yum-friggin'-yum.*

"So, how are things going at work, Jake?" Luca asked.

A teacher was brutally gunned down in front of her entire family, and North Myrtle Beach may have a serial rapist on its hands. "Good," I answered. "Same ol', same ol'."

Luca unwrapped his chopsticks.

Just use a fork, douche bag. I wonder if he can catch a fly in mid-air with those things. I wonder if I can get him to paint my fence and wax my car. Wax on, wax off, dip shit.

"Bree says you're running a lot more these days," Luca said. He flexed his muscles again.

I glanced over at Bree. *I bet she and Aida are having a much better conversation, probably about cramps or something.* "Yeah, I guess."

"You know, you can still take me up on my offer," he said.

"Offer?" I asked, not knowing what the hell he was talking about.

"Taking one of my classes, at the dojo."

The dojo. Should I make a joke about Dojo being Cujo's Asian cousin, or should I make a Cobra-Kai joke. It wouldn't matter, he wouldn't laugh; and Bree, my biggest fan, isn't paying attention. "I don't really think that's for me," I informed him.

Luca rubbed his chin. Jesus, you could bury a dead cat in that dimple. "Oh, trust me, my friend it's for you. It would enhance your strength, your speed, and your hand-eye coordination; it might really help you out in your line of work."

In my line of work I have a gun, you idiot. "Maybe," I pretended to agree.

My cell phone rang, and everyone in the restaurant looked at me like I was an Ebola patient coughing on their plates. "I have to take this," I said, and walked back out into the foyer. "I told you to call me at six-thirty," I whispered. "What the hell took you so long?"

"Sorry," Perkins responded. "I was watching TV."

"Meet me at Duffy's, I'm starving."

"Will do."

I lumbered back to the table with an I'm-so-sorry look on my face. "I have to go. We've had a break in that big case I'm working on."

Luca stood and stuck out his hand. "Aw, that's too bad, buddy, they haven't even brought out our food yet."

I shook Luca's hand and then leaned over to kiss Bree. "Not sure what time I'll be home. I'll give you a call later. Love you."

"Love you, too."

As I climbed into my truck, I wondered if they all bought my act. I just couldn't sit there another minute with that guy. *God, I hope ninjas don't have some secret way of telling a lie from the truth.*

Chapter Twenty-Two

By the time I pulled up across from Duffy's, it was dark. Perkins already had a table out front. He was sitting across from Gwen, and they both had draft beers in front of them. I grabbed a parking spot in front of Georgio's Pizza and joined them.

"Hey, Gwen," I said.

She raised her glass to me and then took a drink. "Needed some rescuing tonight, I hear?"

"Yeah." I looked to Perkins. "Thanks for that. Another minute with ninja banker and I might have had a stroke."

Perkins laughed and sipped his beer.

A waitress walked over. "Can I get you something to drink, Jake?"

"Yes, please. A ginger ale." I looked at Gwen and Perkins. "You two already eat?" They both nodded yes. They had eaten at home. I returned my attention to the waitress. "And Cheryl, bring me the biggest steak you have back there, medium-well. I don't care what kind. Surprise me, and I'll have fries with that."

"Coming right up," Cheryl said with a big smile.

"How long have you been here?" I asked.

"Five minutes," Gwen answered.

"Any leads in *your* case?"

"No, but we're thinking maybe the suspect doesn't have a car and may live in the area," Perkins said. "That would explain the close proximity of the attacks."

"We're also thinking maybe his limp prevents him from walking too far," Gwen added.

"Lint and I were thinking the same thing. We talked to a guy who works next door at Bargain World; they sell the hats in there, and he said they sell them at most flea markets and farmer's markets around the area."

"There's the farmers market over by the library, not too far from here," Perkins pointed out.

"Exactly," I said.

Gwen looked to Perkins. "Maybe we should head over there tomorrow and see if anybody remembers seeing anyone with a limp."

Cheryl sat my ginger ale down in front of me. Perkins downed the last of his beer and held it up. "I'll have another, Cheryl."

"How about you, Gwen?" Cheryl asked.

"I'm good, thanks."

We shared information and bounced ideas off of each other for the next twenty minutes, until my steak and fries arrived. "Oh, that looks good," I announced. "Finally!"

I cut into the steak and was about to put the first bite in my mouth when I noticed a taxi cab pull up and stop near my truck. I paused with my mouth open.

A man climbed from the back seat; he was about six feet tall, average build. He was wearing beige cargo pants and a black T-shirt. I judged he tipped the scales at around two hundred pounds. I laid my fork down. "Hey," I said quietly. Perkins and Gwen looked over. "Check my three o'clock__, the man getting out of the cab."

Perkins and Gwen trained their eyes on him. The man scanned his surroundings, and then walked over to the Pirate's Cove; he was limping.

Six feet tall. Two hundred pounds. Walks with a limp. *Bingo!*

He sat at one of their outside tables. Two of the other tables were occupied; this left one empty.

"Holy shit," Perkins said.

"It can't be," Gwen whispered.

We watched as the waitress brought the man a drink. He smiled and placed a few bills on the table in front of him. Two women in their early twenties walked by. He watched them over his glass as he sipped his drink. He didn't take his eyes off of them until they rounded the corner. The subject probably didn't stare at their asses any more intently than Perkins or I would have; but on the other hand, we didn't fit the description of a local serial rapist to a T.

"I'd stake my badge that's our man—all that's missing is the Beardo," I said. "And he was practically drooling over those two women."

Perkins looked at his watch. "It's only eight o'clock; the other two attacks didn't happen until after midnight."

"We need something to push him along," I pointed out.

"Or some*one*," Gwen said.

We both looked at her. "No," I said. "It's too dangerous."

"Dangerous?" Gwen asked. "I'm a cop with two other cops. Sounds pretty safe to me."

"What do you have in mind?" Perkins asked.

"He hasn't noticed us sitting here," Gwen explained. "You two get up and walk around the side of the building and keep a lookout. I'll get up and cross the street in front of him. If he follows, you follow."

"I don't know," I said cautiously.

"Sounds good to me," Perkins said.

"She can wrap your steak to go, Jake," Gwen joked.

When Cheryl returned to the table she asked, "Is everything okay with your steak, Jake?"

"Yeah, it's good, Cheryl. Can you wrap it up for me?" I pulled a fifty from my money clip and handed it to her. "Here ya go."

"I'll be right back with your change."

"No, keep it, and keep my food inside till I come back for it, please."

A look of concern spread over Cheryl's pretty face. We were regulars and she knew we were cops. "Okay, Jake," she said softly. "Y'all be careful, hear?"

Perkins and I got up from the table. He followed me around the side of the building where we could keep an eye on Gwen and the subject.

We watched as she removed her T-shirt. Underneath she was wearing a blue and white-checkered bikini top. She stood, unbuttoned her shorts and folded the waistband down.

"Wow!" Perkins whispered.

"Really? That's your partner for Chrissakes."

"Yeah. Ain't I lucky?" He looked at Gwen and said.

Gwen took one last sip of her beer, slung her purse strap over her shoulder, and started out across the street. She got to the other side, about three feet in front of our man. She purposely dropped her T-shirt, bent over and picked it up, then preceded down the sidewalk. The subject's eyes watched every move.

"*I'd* follow her," Perkins said.

"Enough," I said.

Just as Gwen got to the parking lot at the end of Main Street, the suspect got up from his chair and counted his money that lay on the table. He grabbed two of the bills, shoved them back into his pocket, and started off down the street. We waited until he was almost to the corner and then began following him.

When he got to the corner of Main and Ocean Boulevard he paused, looked around, and then took a right. He wasn't following Gwen.

"Where's he going?" Perkins asked.

"I have no idea. I'll follow him and you stick with Gwen."

I got to the end of the sidewalk and peeked around the corner. He was gone. Perkins had crossed the street and was just entering the parking lot. I started south on Ocean Boulevard. When I came to the corner of First Avenue, I paused and scanned the area. *Dammit, where did he go?*

Then, out of the corner of my eye, I caught some movement. It was him; he had gone down the First Avenue access. I jogged across the street and made my way through a parking lot; I crouched down behind a row of sea oats and watched him. Gwen was about twenty feet in front of suspect, with her back to him. I couldn't see Perkins from where I was positioned.

Even with his limp, he began walking faster toward her. I shadowed him behind the wall of sea oats.

Just as he began to run, he was pulling something from the side pocket of his pants. I saw Perkins step out from the Main Street access. Gwen was between him and the subject. Gwen spun around just in time to see the man pulling his mask over his face.

"Freeze, police!" Perkins shouted. Only the guy didn't freeze, he dove at Gwen as she was pulling her weapon from her purse.

I drew my weapon and took off running toward them.

The subject rolled over, pulling Gwen on top of him. They were both struggling to gain control of her .38.

Gwen brought her left elbow back into his ribs. Groaning, he let go of her and she rolled off of him. He turned and yanking Gwen's gun from her hand, he aimed it at Perkins. Perkins fired twice. Both rounds hit the man in his right shoulder.

I kicked the pistol from his hand, and he fell back into the sand.

"Are you okay?" I asked Gwen.

"Yes," she answered, climbing to her feet.

"Whore!" the man shouted at her. "You dress like a whore!"

Beach Shoot

It's funny how hard a woman as small as Gwen can kick a guy in the side of the head.

Chapter Twenty-Three

It was around eleven-thirty when I pulled into the driveway, my cold steak sitting in the seat beside me in a Styrofoam container. The house was dimly lit when I walked in, the only light coming from the fixture over the kitchen sink and the glow of the television. The sound on the TV was turned almost all the way down. Bree was asleep on the couch, her favorite throw blanket pulled over her.

I flipped on the kitchen light and went to the fridge to get something to drink.

"Jake?" I heard Bree call out.

I popped the top of my soda can. "Yeah."

"You hungry?"

I pulled a plate out of the cupboard and placed my steak on it. "I grabbed something earlier. I'm going to nuke it." I set the plate in the microwave and hit two minutes and then went into the living room. I sat my soda on the end table and glanced over at the television, Tori Spelling was running through the woods so I looked around for the remote control.

Bree pulled the remote out from under her. "This what you're looking for?"

"Are you sure you don't want to watch Tori run around the forest?" I asked, taking the remote.

"No, that's okay; it really doesn't do that much for me."

I pointed the remote at the TV but couldn't quite bring myself to change the channel; Tori's tatas *were* mesmerizing, as they bounced through the forest like two bowls of Jell-O. "It's ironic that all these young women on Lifetime get chased around by wife beaters, while wearing wife-beaters."

Ding! I went back into the kitchen to fetch my dinner.

When I returned to the living room, Bree was once again sound asleep. I sat in my chair and switched the station over to MeTV; an early episode of *Perry Mason* was on. "I'll bet you a hundred dollars that Mason wins this case," I said.

"I'll pass."

I turned on the lamp next to me and Bree opened her eyes, giving me *that* look. "Sorry, it's too dark. I couldn't see my steak," I informed her.

"Finally got your steak, huh?"

"Yup," I answered, cutting into it.

"I guess you were lucky, getting that call during dinner like you did."

"Yup."

"You caught a bad guy, you got your steak. I guess everything just fell into place for you tonight."

"I guess it did."

"And the streets of North Myrtle Beach are safe once again."

"They are."

I glanced over and Bree was staring at me. She knew the call I got during dinner and the apprehension of a suspected serial rapist was just a coincidence. I gave her a sly smile that let her know I had lied about the call, and that *I* knew *she* knew I had lied. She smiled and closed her eyes. "Sorry," I said. "I just can't eat dinner with a ninja."

Chapter Twenty-Four

Wednesday Morning, Lint and I showed up at the Neil residence on Edgewood Drive, around seven-fifteen. We parked on the opposite side of the street, two houses down, and waited for Paul Neil to get in his car and drive to school. At seven-forty, he did. We pulled out behind him and followed.

On Belle Drive, just before we reached Ninth Avenue, I hit the lights that are hidden in the grill and dashboard of our unmarked unit. Neil looked in his rearview mirror and then pulled to the side of the road. We drove up behind him and stopped.

Lint walked up to the passenger side of the car; I approached the driver's side. Neil already had his window down and was searching through his wallet for his driver's license. I noticed right away the bandage on his left wrist.

"Paul Neil?" I asked.

He halted his search and looked up at me. "Yes."

"Can you step out of the car please, Paul?"

"Did I do something wrong?"

"We just need to ask you a few questions."

Lint walked around the car, pretending to inspect it, which made the boy even more nervous.

Paul handed me his license and then climbed out of the car. I looked at his photo, then at him, and then gave it back to him. When he reached for it I said, "That's quite a bandage there. Must be a pretty bad injury. How did it happen?"

"I did it working on my car yesterday," Paul answered. "What did you need to ask me?"

"We would like you to come with us down to the station," I explained.

"I have to be at school."

"This won't take long. Detective Lint will call the school for you and let them know you'll be a little late."

"Should I call my father?"

"Paul, you're eighteen years old," I explained. "The state doesn't require your father to be present during questioning."

Lint took a shot at playing bad cop. "Listen, Neil, you can follow us down to the station voluntarily and answer a few questions, or we can throw your ass in the back of *our* car, haul you down there, and hold you for twenty-four hours. It's your choice."

"I'll go with you."

"That's what I thought," Lint said, and started back toward the car.

"You drive to the station, and we'll follow you in," I said.

Paul nodded and got back in his car.

When we arrived at the station, we took him right to the interrogation room, I told Lint to go in first because I wanted Paul to be scared; I wanted his throat to dry up.

Lint walked in with a file folder filled with paperwork from the Bowen homicide. He tossed it on the table and took a seat. I watched from a two-way mirror in the observation room.

"Paul, we asked you down here," Lint began, "because we think you may have some information for us about a murder investigation we're conducting."

"Mrs. Bowen's?"

"Yes, Paul. Why don't you tell me everything you know about Mrs. Bowen's murder."

"I don't know anything."

Lint opened the folder and pulled out three photographs, all taken from different angles, of Emily Bowen. All three photos showed her lying in the sand with blood covering the front of her white dress shirt. He placed the photographs in front of Paul. Paul winced and turned his head.

"Horrible, isn't it? A husband, three young children. Those poor kids will grow up without a mom now."

Paul said nothing.

I grabbed a soda from the vending machine and took it, along with a clear plastic cup, into the interrogation room. "Hey, Paul, sorry I took so long, I had to make a phone call." I sat the cup down, opened the soda, and poured some into the cup. "Here, I thought you could use a drink."

"Thank you," Paul said.

I took a seat next to Lint. "I don't know if Detective Lint explained it to you, but we think your friend Jeremy might have had something to do with Mrs. Bowen's murder."

"Jeremy? Why would Jeremy kill Mrs. Bowen?"

"You know it was his car used in the shooting," Lint pointed out.

"Yeah, but it was stolen," Paul argued, and then took a sip of his soda.

"Maybe," I said. "But no one actually saw him during the time of the killing."

"And Mrs. Bowen was failing him in her class, which was causing him to miss football practice," Lint added. "He probably wouldn't have played all year. And failing his senior year could have screwed up his scholarship."

Paul shook his head no. "No way, he wouldn't do it." He took another drink of his soda.

"Paul, do you know anything about the break-in at Grand Strand Photography yesterday morning?" I asked.

"No. How would I know anything about that?"

"Your girlfriend works there, doesn't she, Paul?" Lint asked.

"Yes, I mean no … she used to."

"Did she get along with Alex Caldwell?" I asked.

"I guess."

"Why did she quit?" Lint asked.

Paul shrugged his shoulders.

"Did you go down there a lot to visit with her while she worked?" I asked.

"No. I was only there once, about a year ago when she turned in her application."

"So you never hung around down there?" Lint asked.

"No, never."

Lint and I sat there quietly for a few minutes pretending to go through the paperwork in the folder. Every once in a while, I would point at something and hold up the paper for Lint to see. He would nod his head, and then we would both look up at Paul. There was sweat beading on his brow. Whenever he spoke, his top lip quivered. He was either very scared or was doing one piss-poor Elvis impersonation.

"Can I go now?" Paul asked nervously.

Lint and I looked at each other. "I guess so," I said. "But don't leave town, Paul, we might want to ask you a few more questions."

"I won't," he said, and got up from the table.

Lint pushed the can of soda closer to him. "Don't forget your complimentary soft drink."

Paul picked up the soda can and left the room. I turned to Lint and pointed at the clear plastic cup. "Get that in an evidence bag and get it down to the lab__, see if they can pull some prints off of it. I want to know if the prints match the ones found at Caldwell's place. Also see if they can get any DNA off of the rim. Tell them to put a rush on it. I want the results back yesterday."

Chapter Twenty-Five

The results of the DNA test were back by five o'clock, and they were just what I expected. The DNA from the cup matched the blood traces at the studio. And the prints from Paul Neil's cup matched the prints found on the doorjamb. These findings, along with the injury to Paul's wrist, and the fact that he told us he hadn't been there in over a year, were enough to get a search warrant and a warrant for Paul's arrest.

Lint and I showed up at the Neil residence at seven, along with four uniforms, to execute the warrants.

I knocked on the door; Paul Neil's mother answered.

"Yes?" she asked.

I flashed my badge. "Mrs. Neil?"

"Yes. What's going on?"

I held up the warrant. "Ma'am, we have a warrant to search your residence," I replied, and stepped aside for the other officers to enter.

"You can't just come into my house," she informed me. She turned and hollered for her husband. "Rex!"

I entered last, and Rex Neil met me in the foyer. "What is this?"

I handed him the warrant. "Mr. Neil, is Paul here?"

"Why do you need Paul?" Mrs. Neil asked.

"He's out back, cleaning the pool," Mr. Neil said.

"We also have a warrant for Paul's arrest," I said.

Mrs. Neil buried her face in her husband's chest and began sobbing.

"He's out back," I called to Lint.

As we made our way to the back door we passed two officers, one carrying Paul's laptop, and the other had an iPod and a tablet.

As I reached the door, I could see Paul through the glass skimming the top of the water with a large blue net. He glanced up and saw us coming toward him; he dropped the net and ran toward the back fence.

"Crap!" I yelled. "He's running!"

I followed Paul; Lint turned and sprinted through a gate that led out to the driveway. Paul leaped up on the fence and threw himself over to the ground on the other side. He was up and running by the time I hit the fence. I climbed over and dropped to the other side.

"Paul, stop!" I shouted. He was about twenty yards in front of me, running across a fairway at the Possum Trot Golf Club. The fact that I had lost a few pounds and was running more didn't matter in the least. There was no way I was going to catch him.

Beach Shoot

He ran through a wooded area and on to the next fairway. Through the trees I could see a foursome on the green. When I got to the fairway, I drew my weapon and fired three times into the ground. Paul flinched and stopped for a second. The startled men on the green turned toward me.

"Police!" I shouted. "Stop that kid!"

One of the larger men in the group took off toward Paul. Paul turned and almost made it to the tree line when the golfer tackled him. I holstered my gun and pulled out my cuffs.

Paul Neil was gasping for air when I got to him. "Thanks, pal. Great tackle," I said.

"Don't mention it," the golfer answered. "What did the kid do?"

"Shot a wife and mother of three."

"Shit, if I knew that I would have hit him harder."

I rolled Paul onto his chest and secured his hands behind his back. When I got him to his feet, I said, "Paul Neil, you're under arrest for the murder of Emily Bowen," then I read him his rights.

"I didn't kill anyone!" he cried out.

"That'll be for a jury to decide." I spun him around and we started back toward his house. Lint was at the other end of the fairway, bent over with his hands on his knees.

When we were almost to him, he said, "I'm too old for this."

"No," I corrected him. "you're too fat for this."

Chapter Twenty-Six

Once again, Lint and I sat across from Paul Neil in the interrogation room. This time his hands were cuffed … and I didn't offer him a soda.

"I swear I didn't do it," Paul said for the hundredth time in the last fifteen minutes.

"Paul, we already know you killed her, we just want to know why," Lint said.

"I. Didn't. Kill. Her."

"You were the last person seen driving the car," I said. "Your prints and blood were found at the portrait studio, your prints were also found inside Jeremy's car, and you're the only suspect without an alibi."

"You told us you hadn't been there in a year," Lint reminded him.

"Why did you break in?" I asked.

"Were you afraid he may have gotten a photo of you at the crime scene?" Lint asked.

Paul let out a big sigh and dropped his head. "I broke in to steal pictures he had of Nikki."

"Your girlfriend?" Lint asked.

Paul nodded.

"Why did you want to steal photographs of Nikki?" I asked.

"He took pictures of her … naked pictures," Paul explained.

"She posed for him?" Lint asked.

"Yes, but clothed. When she would go in the next room to change into another outfit, he would take pictures of her through a hole in the wall."

"Where are the photographs?" I asked.

"I gave them to Nikki."

"What does any of this have to do with Emily Bowen?" Lint asked.

"Nothing! I'm telling you, I don't know anything about her murder. Why would I kill her?"

"I don't know, Paul." I answered. "Did you go there to shoot Caldwell and accidentally shot Mrs. Bowen?"

"I didn't go there, I was home," Paul insisted. "Can I please have something to drink?"

"Sure," I said and got up from the table. When I got to the vending machine, I glanced into the lounge Nicole Irvine and her mother were sitting with the Neil's. When Nicole saw me, she got up and walked over. Her mother followed.

"Can I see Paul?" Nicole asked.

I looked over her shoulder and saw the Neils approaching.

"Not right now, Nikki."

"Detective, what's going on?" Mr. Neil asked. "No one will tell us anything."

"Mr. Neil, if you could wait in the lounge, I'll be in as quick as I can to talk to you and your wife. I have a few questions for you, as well."

"I'm calling my attorney, Stellar. Don't ask Paul another question until he gets here."

"Paul is an adult, Mr. Neil. If he requests an attorney, we will let you know." I turned to Nicole, and motioned toward Merle's office. "Can you come in here for a minute, Nikki? I would like to talk to you."

"Can my mom come in, too?" she asked.

"If you want her to." I opened Merle's office door and they went in. "Have a seat," I said, pointing to the leather sofa.

"Is Paul going to jail?" Nikki asked.

I ignored the question and sat on the edge of Merle's desk. "Nikki, Paul told us he broke into Caldwell's studio to steal nude photos of you. Is that true?"

The look on Mrs. Irvine's face told me that she knew nothing about it. "Oh my God," she said. "Nikki, is this true?"

"Yes," Nicole responded. "He had to break in; Alex was going to put the pictures on the Internet."

"He told you he was putting them on the Internet?" I asked.

Nicole nodded. "He told me that if I didn't sleep with him that he would make sure everyone saw the pictures. Paul had to do it. He did it to protect me. How much trouble is he in because of me?"

"This isn't your fault, Nikki," Mrs. Irvine said, and put her arm around her daughter.

"Nikki, did anyone else know that Caldwell had these pictures?" I asked.

"No, I didn't tell anyone."

"Did you ever go on photo shoots with Caldwell?"

"Yes, all the time, but just on the weekends."

"Were you supposed to be at the Bowen shoot, before you quit?"

"Yes."

"Would anyone else have known about the appointment?"

"Just me and Alex." She paused for a moment and looked at her mother. "But, last Friday, I walked into my bedroom and my father was looking through my appointment book. He said he found it lying on the kitchen counter and was just returning it to my room."

"Were the locations of your shoots written in the planner?"

"Yes."

I looked to Mrs. Irvine. "Your husband told us that the three of you went to breakfast Sunday morning. Is that true?"

"Yes," she replied. "Several people saw us there."

"Do you remember exactly what time you were there?"

Mrs. Irvine reached into her purse for her cell phone. "I can look," she said, thumbing through her recent call log. "My husband called for us to pick him up at … ten twenty-seven."

"Pick him up? Pick him up from where?"

"He went for a run. He was going to meet us at the diner, but he called and said he had twisted his ankle, and for us to pick him up."

"Where did you pick him up?"

"Right under the water tower." She dropped her phone back into her purse.

"Mrs. Irvine, where is your husband right now?"

"He … he went outside to have a cigarette. Why?"

I pushed myself away from the desk and walked through Merle's door. As I got to my desk, Mr. Irvine came back into the station.

I stared at him, and he stared back. His body seemed to relax and his shoulders dropped slightly. "It was an accident," he said.

Chapter Twenty-Seven

When I got home, I swung the door closed behind me and called out, "Honey, I'm home." No one replied. There was an open bottle of Lambrusco on the table.

I walked around the house. "Bree!" I called out. I went into the living room; the television was off. The patio lights were on, and I could see Bree through the window, swimming around in the pool. She had a glass of wine in her hand. She was wearing the purple bikini, the one she never wore in public.

I went to the bedroom, removed my clothes, and put on my bathing suit. On my way to the back door I grabbed the bottle of wine.

"Refill?" I asked.

Bree smiled. "Yes, please."

She swam over to the edge, and I sat down on the step with my feet in the water. Bree lifted her glass and I topped it off. I sat the bottle on the concrete edging next to me.

"We wrapped up the investigation today," I said matter-of-factly.

"I know."

"How do you know?"

"I can see it in your face."

I leaned forward, she rose up, and we kissed. "I love you," I said.

"I love you, too. Was it Colonel Mustard, with the lead pipe, in the library?"

"It was Nicole Irvine's father."

Bree's jaw dropped. "Why?"

"Alex Caldwell had nude pictures of Nicole, and he was trying to blackmail her for sex."

"Sounds like a real piece of shit."

"Yeah, he won't get what he deserves, though__, he'll cop a plea. Irvine will probably do twenty for the killing."

"What does any of that have to do with the teacher?"

"Irvine overheard his daughter and her boyfriend discussing the pictures. He looked in Nicole's appointment book to see where Caldwell was going to be that morning and went there to kill him. He told his wife he was going for a run. He ran all right__, to the Davis house, and took Jeremy's car. He had heard the kids talk about not needing a key to turn the ignition. He fired, missing Caldwell with all three shots, but accidently hit Emily Bowen. After the shooting he ditched the car, ran a few blocks, and then called his wife to pick him up, claiming that he had hurt his ankle."

"Wrong place at the wrong time," Bree commented.

"That's about the size of it."

"And then he broke into the studio to get the pictures?"

"No, it was Paul Neil who broke in to get the pictures."

"Did he get them?"

"Yes … and anything he didn't get, we will. They're clearing out his studio as we speak."

Bree set her glass on the side of the pool and pushed off the step, doing the back stroke across the water. Her breasts heaved and flexed with each stroke. "Come on in," she said. "The water's great."

It looked great. I slid off the step into the water. "Warm," I said. I made my way toward her.

"Aida called earlier."

I put my arms around her and kissed her neck. "Oh yeah."

"She said her and Luca felt bad that you missed out on dinner last night, so they've invited us to go out with them Saturday night."

Crap!

The End

Coming August 2015

Return to Dunquin Cove

Coming Winter 2015

Double Trouble

From the Tales of Dan Coast

Sleeping Dogs Lie

From the Tales of Dan Coast

A mystery set in the Florida Keys follows Dan Coast, an unlicensed private detective of sorts, as he is hired to find the missing boyfriend of a woman who herself soon ends up missing. When someone from the woman's past unexpectedly shows up at Dan's home, with a story of faked deaths and missing life insurance money; Dan along with his sidekick Red set out to find the money, and the woman.

ISBN: 978-0-9883503-0-4

Ocean Floors

From the Tales of Dan Coast

The second installment in the Dan Coast series, Ocean Floors, is a tale of mystery and possible romance when a chance meeting with a beautiful young woman leads Dan and his trusted sidekick Red down a road of murder and kidnapping. Join Dan and Red as they try to solve the murder while searching for a missing friend.

ISBN: 978-0-9894877-0-2

Impaled

An Adirondack Short Story

Eric Stone is an investigator with The Town of Webb Police Department. Chuck Little is Head Ranger at the Nick's Lake campground. An unlikely duo, together they work to solve a murder that mimics a spree of gruesome murders taking place years earlier. Is it a copycat, or has the murderer resurfaced after all of these years? Join Stone and Little as they piece together the clues to solve this mystery taking place in the small village of Old Forge in the Adirondack Mountains.

North Murder Beach

A Jake Stellar Novel

The first installment of the story of North Myrtle Beach police detective, Jake Stellar. The spring bike rallies have ended, the spring breakers have all gone back to school, and the summer tourist season is a few weeks away. What better time for a police officer to take a nice quiet relaxing week off from work? That's what Jake Stellar had in mind. That is until someone from his past resurfaces to remind him of a terrible secret he has spent years trying to forget. In North Murder Beach, a story of revenge, Jake is unwillingly and violently forced to confront his secret from his past.

ISBN: 978-0-9894877-1-9

The Coast of Christmas Past

From the Tales of Dan Coast

Coast of Christmas Past is the third book in the Dan Coast series of books. Dan Coast is all set to spend Christmas just the same way he has every year for the past few years; alone and drunk. But when uninvited, unexpected guests arrive and throw a wrench into his holiday plans he is forced to sober up (slightly), and throw on a smile. Just when it seems nothing else could go wrong, a close friend is injured in what appears, to the police, to be a drug deal gone bad. Dan Coast and his sidekick, Red jump into action to find the truth while their friend lies unconscious in the hospital.

ISBN: 978-0-9894877-3-3

The Man in Room Number Four

When a mysterious stranger arrives in the small coastal town of Dunquin Cove, Maine it appears as though Claire and her young son, Mica's prayers have been answer.

But who is he, and why is he really here? Join Claire and her guests at the Colsome House Bed and Breakfast as they piece together the mystery of the Man in Room Number Four.

ISBN: 978-0-9894877-2-6

Ship of Fools

From the Tales of Dan Coast

Ship of Fools is the fourth book in The Tales of Dan Coast series and begins where Coasts of Christmas Past left off. Find out how Dan deals with the death of a young friend, while looking into the disappearance of a new friend's sister. Join Dan, Red, and Skip as they fumble their way through a new mystery.

ISBN: 978-0-9894877-4-0